Can You Feel What I'm Saying?:
An Erotic Anthology

James Earl Hardy

dedication: To all the boiz I've loved *and* lusted before ...

CONTENTS

acknowledgments: A hat tip and bow to ... the Creator, my parents, my blood and bond families, my Advisory Board (La Marr Jurelle Bruce, Don Gagnon, James Grant, Darnell L. Moore, Quincey J. Roberts, Cornell Sewell, Nathan Simmons, and Corey Yarbrough), and the fans worldwide. Thanks for your love, support, affirmations, prayers—and patience!

THE LAST PICTURE. SHOW.

BuTay had had enough.

You can't fake the fuck, a nutt is a must—especially if you're doin' it on camera. If the one you're with isn't bringing out the freak in you, you gotta do whatever and think about *whoever* to bring it. Don't let up that you've been let down. Keep a, *ahem*, straight face, and make the camera believe you. 'Cause the camera never lies.

It's not the first time he's had to put on a fuckin' happy face (or is that a happy fuckin' face?), but it will be the last. This is it for him. *This is it*. His last picture. Yes, he's said it before and he's meant it before, but this time the decision has been made for him.

This Big D. You guessed it, aka Big Dick. With a name like that if he wasn't doing porn he'd be a pimp, a rapper, or some combination thereof (they are more often than not all-in-one these days). He's a walking caricature. An obnoxious rope-a-dope chain swinging from his neck, diamond studs in each ear, silver rings on his right fingers and gold on his left (including the thumbs), and a grill that caps his upper row. Dipped in ink on his right thigh (something in Chinese), his left arm (something in Japanese), down his spine (a scorpion), and above his navel (an arrow pointing downward with *Da Shyt* above it). And the splotchy mark just below his right shoulder blade? Apparently the result of a drive-by in Compton, where he fulfilled his gangsta score card as a drug dealer.

The main attractions are the brick house bod, that big ol' dick (a ruler by six and three-quarter inches), and the sack (dubbed "Monster's Balls"). Ever since he exploded (pun intended) on the scene a couple of years ago, he's been the talk. The pubic can't get enough of him.

BuTay thought he wouldn't be able to get enough of him, too. The man is *f-f-f-fine* and, from what he had seen, could fuck up a storm. And, BuTay felt rather honored: he would be the first man Big would do on screen (the jury is still out on whether he has done it off). Several studios—FreakDawg, PitBull, and Enrique Cruz—tried to woo him, but he said yes to Full Moons and it's president/director/producer, Ernest Jamison aka EJ, because EJ could promise him the person ... no, the *ass* he's always wanted to nail.

But whatever excitement BuTay felt disintegrated when they met.

BuTay has three "hell-2-the-naw" commandments: no drugs, no bareback, and no raining on his face. And in a world where the three often go hand in hand, that he's been able to avoid them all is something of a miracle.

So it's a rather poetic form of justice that he would be faced with all three today.

When they were in the "dressing/make-up room" (a large walk-in utility closet), Big decided to light up a joint. "Wanna puff?"

Not, "Do you mind if I smoke?" But, at least he offered. He has manners.

"No thanks."

"Mo' fo' me, then."

Good thing he's one of those artists who frowns on intimacy (i.e., kissing, hugging, cuddling); BuTay wouldn't have to inhale the stank on his lips.

As they rehearsed—choreographing their movements so that they'd always be on camera and on cue—Big had the audacity to ask: "You mind if we do this raw, dawg?" He'd done it bareback with women.

But not with BuTay. "Yes I do."

"You ain't gotta worry. I got me."

Yeah, you got you; who's gonna have me?

He kept pleading his case. "Ain't no problem. I can pull out befo' I blow."

"You won't be pullin' in if you're not covered."

He shrugged. "A'ight, a'ight, son. No prob."

Uh-huh. I know it won't be.

And after almost a half hour of some very uninspired pumpin' and pushin', it seemed as if he was about to blow— and would no doubt be springing forth his seed on BuTay's face. It was bad enough BuTay had to listen to this motherfucker have sex with *himself* ...

"This shit is hot, ain't it?" "No doubt, money." "I'm committin' a genocide on this azz, huh?" "You sho' is, dawg."

Yawn.

... and that he couldn't keep his shit up. Twice during the fuck scene BuTay had to go down on him.

He wasn't about to let Big use his face as a towel. If BuTay wanted a facial, he'd go to a spa.

And it was obvious that, despite BuTay's protests, EJ was fine with letting it happen. And why wouldn't he be: Big is an executive producer on *Big's Big Break*, a credit that EJ had always denied BuTay despite his being his biggest star and making over a million dollars for him in two years. This bit of information was revealed by Big minutes before the shoot began—and you know that left a *very* bitter taste in BuTay's mouth. When confronted, EJ at first denied it but then dismissed it as "just business." Uh-huh. And the expression he wore as Big ejected his dick and went for the condom broadcasted the same sentiment.

It was in that moment that BuTay's whole career flashed before his eyes. His butay had seen better days. *Much* better days.

BuTay—or Evan, as his parents named him—didn't fall into the biz because he was trying to feed a drub habit. Or needed a warm bed to sleep for a night or two. He wasn't molested or sexually abused as a child and is exorcising those demons by playing with himself and others in public. Nor was he hard up for money. Or hard up.

He answered an ad in *HX Magazine*—to be an office manager. He was a junior at NYU pursuing a degree in creative writing (a career choice that disappointed his parents). He never managed an office but the work hours fell on days he wasn't in class and the position didn't require you to have experience. It stated: "Charismatic cutie with bootie needed to oversee clerical operations, Thurs-Sat, 1pm-9pm."

Charismatic cutie with bootie. That was him.

He got the job because he was the only Negro out of the dozen candidates that applied. That's who EJ wanted all along, but he couldn't very well include that in the ad. Why any of the white boys showed up was a mystery: even a porn outsider like Evan was aware of EJ's predeliction for dark meat.

Which is why Evan wore the tightest pair of jeans to the "interview." One look was all it took: After dismissing all the vanilla, they sat in a corner of his Lower East Side loft that also functioned as his office, where EJ made one offer Evan couldn't refuse—and another that he could.

After agreeing on his pay and going over his duties, EJ walked him out, zeroing in on his backside. "You oughta be in pictures with an ass like that."

Evan figured that most Black men he laid that line on were appreciative. Not him. "I don't think so."

EJ was thrown by the response. "You don't think so? Why not?"

Why not. As in, *Why wouldn't you want to since I, the white man, said you would be good in them, I know everything, and I know what's best for everyone, including you.*

"Because I know what's best for me and that's not it."

"Well ... have you ever been photographed nude? You might change your mind once you see how beautiful you are."

Beautiful. Evan had heard that from many a white man eager to get into his pants. "Don't you mean how beautiful my ass is?"

"Uh, well, yeah," he admitted with nervous laughter.

"I'll be keeping my clothes on."

He kept that promise—for a year. EJ continued his quest to convince Evan to act (suggesting that he ease into the biz by doing a solo scene with a dildo) and become his lover (needlessly patting his ass as if they were on a basketball team and brushing behind him *very* slowly). And many of the actors who came through Full Moons' doors *really* tempted him to take off his clothes, on and off camera. The boiz—Black, Latino, and Blatino—were too fuckin' fine for words; most flirted with him, some pushed up (literally), and a few requested, with dick in hand, that he "fluff" them before they went on camera. It also didn't help that EJ sometimes filmed in the upstairs bunker; the sounds and smells were hard to ignore—and made *him* hard. But he resisted and never saw anyone outside the office; he didn't want to get a reputation for sleeping with his employer's actors. He knew that if he took just one baby step in that direction, he would be pulled all the way in.

It's just a matter of time, many told him, *before you take that dive.* Unfortunately for EJ, it didn't happen in a film he directed. It was on a Monday before class, and Evan dropped by the office to pick up his paycheck. EJ was helping cast *Ruffnecks &*

Rednecks; he and Jess Cunningham, the president of Good Ol'
Boy Productions and the director/producer/writer of *R & R*
(yeah, believe it or not, porn flicks *do* have scripts, even if they
aren't longer than a dozen pages), had seen 50 actors over two
days and no one had captured Jess' eye.

But when Jess saw Evan walk in the door, the search was
over.

"Well, it's about time!" Jess cried like Anthony Perkins after he first lays eyes on Diana Ross in *Mahogany*. He swooped
down on Evan like a vulture and ushered him over to a couch
where one of the proposed rednecks—a Larry The Cable Guy
clone wearing black jeans and a white muscle tee—sat.

"He's not here to audition," EJ dryly stated. Evan frowned
at him. *That's right, white man, speak for me like you always think
you can.*

"Are you kidding me? He's *perfect*." He turned to Evan.
"You are Benji."

EJ did the introductions (the "redneck" in question going by the name Peeter Paul), after which Evan politely informed Jess, "I'm not an actor."

"With *that* face? *That* body?" Jess's eyes dropped down.
"And *that* junky trunk?"

Oh no. Another wannabe-hip white boy in our midst. At least
EJ didn't pretend to be down or get it; he left the Blackisms to
the ones who know and do them the best.

"You are Benji," he repeated, just in case it was missed
the first time.

Evan didn't have the chance to respond—Jess handed
him a copy of the script and pointed to the description of Ben-
jamin aka Benji, highlighted in orange: *Black as midnight, very
thick full lips, light lust-filled eyes, short haircut, medium muscular
build, ass like a donkey.*

It was border-line racist. Yet ... *That's me*, Evan thought to himself.

"*You* are the man I have always dreamed of bringing this character to life. Please, *please* read for me," Jess pleaded.

Evan glanced at EJ, who shrugged.

"Hey Boss, can you give me a lift?" Evan directed towards Peeter Paul, whose eyes were glued to Evan's ass.

"Uh ... " Jess began, cautiously. "Can you be more ... ethnic?"

"More what?"

"You know, more ... more ... ghetto." Uh-huh. *You mean more niggerish, like the slave master said in the movie Drum, right?*

"I didn't grow up in a ghetto." And he didn't. Coral Springs is a way-upper-middle class enclave 20 miles south of Detroit. Like his father (a pediatrician) and mother (an insurance adjustor), his neighbors earned close to seven figures annually, sent their children to the Jack & Jill club and to HBCU's, and vacationed on Martha's Vineyard in the summer and the Poconos in the fall. So his vocabulary wasn't sprinkled with "yo," "ain't," and the ever-popular "nigga," even after living in Bed-Stuy for three years.

"Oh." Jess was clearly surprised (or was that disappointment?).

But Evan knew just what he wanted and gave it to him.

"I'll give it a try." He winked at EJ; EJ knew he was playing with him. Evan's posture became slumped. He switched to his DON'T FUCK WITH ME mask, which he had to perfect living in da 'hood. He glared at Peeter Paul, who leaned back. His voice went from tenor to baritone, with a little scratch in the throat for added affect. "Ya Boss. Can ya gimme a lif'?"

Evan never thought he'd see someone do it, but Jess actually jumped for joy. *"That's it!"*

Both Evan and EJ smiled.

Jess paced, clapping furiously. "We'll fly you down to Atlanta next Wednesday. You can stay at my home. I'm sure EJ won't mind doing without you for a couple of days ... "

"Sorry, but I'm not your man," Evan interrupted.

"But you *are*," he replied, still in step.

"I can't."

"Yes, you *can*."

"It's not something I want to do."

"You'll want to."

Jess ignored the no. He called Evan on his cell. He called him at his apartment. He e-mailed him. He sent flowers to the office, even a "flesh-o-gram" (a buffed brother who disrobed to a hip-hop version of "There's No Business Like Show Business"). But it was that "final, *final* offer" he put on the table (Jess presented him with five) that changed his mind.

Evan wasn't looking forward to being pawed and plowed by a ratty ragamuffin named (what else?) Bubba, who looked like he just rolled out from *under* the trailer park (balding, bearded, and beer-bellied), but he managed to not reveal he was totally creeped out by the clammy hands, body odor, and that monstrously hairy back (after all, it's called *acting*). As it turned out, once he and Bubba got into it, it was a hell of lot better than he thought it could be: The man wasn't a bad kisser; devoured the dick like his life depended on it; had somethin' to work with himself (nine inches with a decent width); and *worked* BuTay rather nicely in four different positions (bent over, doggie, on his back, and Evan's favorite, sitting down). Add the thick humidity of a sweltering Atlanta afternoon, the incessant buzz of the gnats and mosquitos, the rusty rickety red and blue pick-up truck, the ripped stained mattress, BuTay chewing on Bubba's pink fuzzy balls, Bubba gnawing on that ass hole as his scruffy beard scratches Bu-

Tay's unblemished booty, the thump of the gun rack (hooked to the back window and holding an AK-47 rifle) as BuTay bumped his ass down and Bubba pumped his dick up, BuTay decorating Bubba's face (Bubba insisted) and Bubba polishing BuTay's ass with his own cream ... and you had the makings of a *semen*al moment in porn, a moment that Smutmeister, the critic for the on-line porn zine *Get Off*, described as "one of the most repulsive *and* hottest fucking scenes ever." Evan *was* repulsed by the whole experience, yet that was the key to making it so hot. It was nasty sex with a nasty man—and he made it even *nastier*, upping the *eeeeeeew* factor with some inspired improvisation (snacking on Bubba's crusty toes and catching the sweat dropping off his forehead with his tongue), moaning his lines with bone-chilling sureness (*"Rock me wit' dat cock, Papa Bear, yeeeaaah!"* and *"Bang ma big black bu-tay, Bubba!"*), and yodeling (it would become his celluloid hallmark). And, any time he began to lose the lust Jess recognized in his eyes—or the breakfast he had eaten several hours before they filmed—he thought of the $10,000 cashier's check he'd receive at the end of the day's shoot.

What people do for money ...

The *pre*verted passion BuTay exuded was so convincing that he earned the GayVN award (the Oscar of queer porn) for Best Supporting Actor, the first Negro victor (the voters must've "forgotten" he was *R & R*'s star). Smutmeister christened him "the Hattie McDaniel of Gay Smut" (since Smutmeister quoted him as declaring "I'd rather play a ho' than be one" and BuTay wore a stars and bars bandana on his head in the film, the comparison was convenient though misguided) and his triumph was heralded as "a new day for the industry." What that "new day" was supposed to look like and bring with it no one ever explained although the implication was clear to most: Black actors had "arrived" and would receive commensurate pay, perks, and promotion. Of course, that day never came, but BuTay did become the new "it" boy. He made two more *R & R* flicks, getting *very* trashy with Shane, a Toby Keith twin, in a truck stop bathroom (their filthiest scenes: Shane splashing Coors on and licking it off of BuTay's chest, back and ass; BuTay cleaning out the cheese clumped under Shane's foreskin with his tongue; and Shane sticking his lit cigar into BuTay's ass—and BuTay *smoking* it); and reuniting with Bubba for a barnyard frolic that was almost as nauseating as their first romp (wrestling naked in a giant aluminum tub full of slop; BuTay inhaling and licking Bubba's hairy, smelly armpits; and Bubba using BuTay's bootay as the bowl and inserting a carrot, an ear of corn, a cucumber, and slithers of tomato to create the ultimate garden salad). The former performance brought BuTay a Best Actor GayVN nomination.

Then the make of white man selected as his co-star improved *dramatically* (Black men aren't usually paired with white men who are "Double A," or All-American types), beginning with the *International BuTay* series, which chronicled his sexploits with men of different European backgrounds (Russian, Israeli, French, Spanish, and British) during a gymnastics competition (naturally, BuTay got pummeled on the pommel horse), Foreign Legion boot camp (the four soldiers had a ball digging a trench in his ass), rugby and soccer matches (the boys from Paris and Madrid had the thighs—and dicks—of steel, and BuTay throroughly enjoyed squeezing and pleasing them all), and rehearsal for an all-male production of *Hamlet* (the tag line: "Ay, *He's* The Rub!"). In *Forgive Me Father*, he confessed his sins ("I'm a homo and I'm going to hell") to a priest (the very brawny and beary Arpad Miklos), who committed a few sins on and inside of him—in the confessional. But *Bangin' Black Boyz 'n Bootz* was the across-the-board fave: his Timberlands were literally knocked off his feet by the very endowed

Chad Hunt, who attempted to reconstruct BuTay's rectum by violently banging him up against a sanding table, hung over a step ladder, and on the roof of a pile driver, as BuTay begged for both mercy *and* more. Their ferocious fuckfest deservedly won the GayVN for Best Couple.

However, he didn't make the bulk of his green on the screen but on the road. He appeared at gay clubs and public events (from the "White Party" circuit to the Folsom Street Fair) where he'd autograph copies of his dvds; in two instances caught on film, he signed one fan's chest and another's dick (he refused to dance or strip for cash; the thought of doing either made him feel ... dirty). He also offered his services to a very select clientele as an escort. Men in the sex industry have adopted that title when in reality they are nothing but prostitutes, but he actually escorted his callers (which included three closeted, married Republican Senators) to banquets, concerts and conferences, where he was often introduced as their "personal assistant" (and, in one instance, "son"). His profile in *A Man's Man*, a tasteful flesh rag that caters to the wealthy, specifically said that "sex is not a part of the package," but he would sleep in the same bed and sometimes participated in intimate play (massage, rimming, frottage, blow jobs, mutual jerk-off), depending on the man (i.e., if they didn't totally gross him out, which was most of the time). He was paid $1000-$2500 for a night and $3000-$5000 for a weekend, *not* including first class airfare (be it on a commercial airline, their private jet, or an Acela express train), ground transportation (his preference: black stretch limos), meals (an Apple marketing V.P. in Simi Valley hired food and wine connoisseur Ted Allen of *Queer Eye for the Straight Guy* to prepare a romantic dinner, midnight snack, and breakfast for two), and "miscellaneous" (such as a clothing allowance for the appropriate wardrobe, be it a tux, a linen suit, silk pajamas, tennis wear, golf gear, even speedos and sandals for the beach). Everyone was more than generous, but some were *really* big spenders. A forensic biologist in Reston treated him to a cruise to the Bahamas, where they stayed for three nights and four days at the swanky JW Marriott (BuTay couldn't get over the giant, crystal chandeliers and the gold embossed door knobs, handles and faucets). He joined a Tony-winning Broadway musical producer on a two-week excursion to Sydney, Amsterdam and Munich. He received $15,000 in cash and gifts (including a custom-made eel skin coat and a 42-inch plasma screen television) from a cardiologist in Portland. An entertainemnt lawyer in Beverly Hills sent him a Mercedes; one of *his* clients, a semi-closeted Oscar winning actor, did the same (he sold them both).

Of course, there were a few extraordinary cases where he did more than just show up. He participated in a celebrity date auction sponsored by COLT Men to benefit the pediatric AIDS ward at Los Angeles Memorial Hospital. He was "won" by Stefan and Eduardo Franz-Lopez, a professional body-building inter-national (Latvian and Ecuadorian) couple. He doesn't know if the wild evening (very passionate sex on the beach, by a fire, under the moonlight) they spent together was worth the $7,650 they bid, but it was for him (it was his first—and still his best—menage a trois). He earned $5,000 as a model for a Tom of Finland exhibit in San Francisco, where several of the artist's works were brought to life. He was captured being fucked in a locker room by one white man while another looked on. As BuTay stood with both his head and dick positioned to the left and arched upwards, Baron was seated behind him with his dick half-way up inside BuTay, focusing on the ass while clutching BuTay around the torso with his right arm and squeezing a tube of what was marked vaseline (it was actually toothpaste) with his left. The shoot was supposed to take less than an hour but dragged on for close to two. An exact replica of the drawing was needed (one detail was changed: it wasn't done bareback) and something was always in the wrong position: BuTay's ass, Baron's dick, BuTay's neck, Baron's left arm, BuTay's right shoulder, Baron's hair, BuTay's right elbow, Baron's left eye, BuTay's nose, Baron's left thumb, BuTay's right pinky, Baron's shorts (which were pulled down between his waist and knees). While it was supposed to *look* like they were fucking they weren't *supposed* to be fucking, and BuTay and Baron kept messing up the shot because it was feeling so good. Getting in was no problem; getting in and remaining completely still was. Baron was expected to get excited but not *too* excited, and it was *hard* for him (his dick) not to—and it was *hard* for BuTay (his ass) not to, too. Even if Baron just moved his dick a quarter inch, BuTay couldn't help but react and move his ass along (it also impressed BuTay that Baron could hold an erection for much of that time). BuTay also found it hard not to stick out his tongue, unpurse and lick his lips, and hold his dick in check. Just when the photographer was about to lose the few strands of hair on his head, they finally nailed it—and then Baron went on to nail *it*. BuTay shot his own load, as did Kristoff, the voyeur, who remarked: "That was the best almost fuck I've ever seen in my life."

And let's not forget the televangelist in Fort Lauderdale, who threw a costume party in which two lucky guests won a raffle to participate in a foursome—while the other eight guests watched. You can find clips of it on ForbiddenVideos and XTube, with BuTay by a pool sucking off Jason Vorhees, being sucked off by Captain Hook, and getting fucked by Predator. The nine-hour fiesta, which included a buffet where the Green Lantern, Spider-Man, Batman & Robin, Pinhead, The Lone Ranger, Freddy Kreuger, and The Grinch doused him with soy and duck sauce and ate sushi off of him, brought him a hefty $40,000.

Evan was having fun. Lots of fun. Maybe *too* much fun. He never imagined being a part of the Triple X club and at times still couldn't believe that he was. He accepted that, at this time in his life, he was fucking for a living and that there was nothing inherently wrong with that. It was easy money— he could shoot a scene a day (more like three to five hours) and make enough to cover all his bills for several months. He loved to fuck, loved to *be* fucked, so if someone wanted to shell out thousands of dollars a pop for him to get popped, why not? He paid off his student loans and became a home owner at 23 (a power move that made his parents proud). He visited countries and met people he probably never would have. And his time was his own—he could devote days, sometimes an entire month to writing that Great American Novel he'd been carrying around since he was 12. He didn't have to punch a time clock or ask for permission to take a break. He was his own boss, others had to work around his schedule—if he chose to have one.

But he knew that, one day, there'd be no more gravy for the mashed potatoes—but was somewhat taken aback by the reason why.

There's an unwritten but understood rule Black actors have historically operated under in gay porn: *Once you go black you can never come back.* White actors can fuck and be fucked by every color of the rainbow on film but Black men usually have to choose a side. This is why you will probably never see a Matthew Rush (yeah, he's a Negro), Jay Black, Dred Scott, Jeremy Tucker, or Simon Cox paired up with someone who doesn't have a tan courtesy of a salon or the beach (that includes your Latinos Blancos). You can start out on the black-hand side and venture over (after all, what colored man *doesn't* want to be with a white boy?), but once you cross that white line you fall out of flavor. You're no longer "exclusive." You are no longer "one of ours," as BuTay heard more than one white man say to him.

His membership in the Snow Patrol was revoked (and immediately passed on to Diesel Washington) with the release of *BuTay-Liscious,* his Full Moons debut. His contract was up with Good Ol' Boy and, while Jess pushed to extend it for another nine films, he wasn't interested (they did issue one last title—*Black Puddin: BuTay's Best*). After being smothered by white men for three years, he wished to get Black to his roots. He took a *lot* of flak from folk, Black gay folk especially, in and outside the industry, working for a company with such a "questionable" name, for *only* getting fucked by white men on screen, and for being a snow queen (which was totally untrue; Bubba was his very first white man and he always said the only way he'd sleep with one is if he were paid to). He had never really cared about what others thought, but being branded a traitor to the race, a spook, Mandingo, and house nigger by his own bothered him. It also ruined his love life: while marriage proposals from white men presented themselves weekly, the brothers weren't calling at all, except those who wished to brag they bagged a porn star (he could smell 'em a mile away). Even some of the cutiez at Full Moons who had become friends through him shade.

BuTay could have "retired": between the films, photo shoots, public appearances, gifts, and escort service, he'd clocked nearly a half million, most of it undeclared and sitting in various stocks, money market, CD, high yield savings and checking accounts (he received sound financial tips from an investment banker who waived his consulting fee after BuTay waved his ass in his face and up on the dick for three hours; it was one of the few times BuTay had sex with a Black man during that whiteout period). But he felt not obligated, not indebted ... *grateful* to EJ. The man was the first to offer to put him in pictures, gave him his first big break (indirectly), and remained a close friend and confidant after he left to become part of the Good Ol' Boy family, advising him on what moves to take to make the the most of his fourteen minutes of fame.

So, to take ahold of his own image (and as sort of a quid pro quo), BuTay joined Full Moons as a contracted star player. Truth be told, BuTay was actually coming to EJ's rescue: after releasing a string of moderate successes, Full Moons was on the brink of bankruptcy. EJ needed some new blood to pump some new life into the company, and pairing some of his somewhat popular performers with the enormously popular BuTay could do just that. BuTay's salary dropped considerably (from $22,500 to $3000) and the escort service dried up (the white men no longer wanted to pay for the privilege) but he didn't mind; he was, in a sense, coming back home, and his piece of mind and happiness were more important than money. While there was some initial resistance to his addition to the roster (a few refused to work with him and one actor, Masta Ace, snapped on him to his face: "Them white boys don't want yo' azz no mo', so you come to us, huh?"), that changed once they saw how uninhibited and insatiable he was (he had been storing up the *real* freakiness for some time and was finally able to let it all out). Pretty soon the other actors were jockeying for position to be next in line, including Masta Ace—not to mention the "down low" hip-hop artists, R&B singers, and professional ball players, who usually requested his cumpany after a concert, awards show, or game. BuTay purchased a special cell just for them, their reps, or their boiz to call, clocking several g's per appointment (after a few tried to use their own ice as payment, he required the funds be wired into a special account or the cash be placed in his hands before the do went down). He was also the "headliner" (bobbing on at least a dozen knobs) one year at FreakOut, a mid-week underground sex-cursion for closeted Black male celebs (to keep gossip ghouls like Wendy Williams at bay, the dates and city are switched each year).

He's still BuTay but is also affectionately referred to as EOA (Equal Opportunity Azz) by the Children, for just about every color under the sun, moon, and stars has had him (on film, anyway). His FM catalog includes: *Rican Rump Shakers* (the phat-dicked Phat Daddy pulverized him in the last car of a northbound #1 train on an early Sunday morning); *Dominican Dick Down* (the "J" Crew—Johnathan, Jaime, Jiminez, Jermaine, and Joey—jumped his ass as part of an initiation, then took turns jumping *in* his ass); the *"My ____ Guy"* Trilogy, in which three fans were selected by BuTay to be his co-star (the *Jamiacan* was Rowdy Boy; the *Brazilian,* Mighty Manuel Montez; and the *Arabian,* Kaseem the Dream who, as the dvd cover proclaimed, "knows how to make BuTay scream!"); *My Chocolate Fortune Cookie* (with the delectable Brandon Lee showing BuTay how to prepare and *do* the chop suey); *Cowboyz & Indians* (Chief Beef, a six-foot, 240-pound hulking Navaho with a braided ponytail that reaches his waist, lassoed BuTay 'round the waist—and up the ass); and the TLA Video #1 hits *Two Gays Can Play That Game* (in which the studio's first white actors—identical twin brothers Kain and Able—played the sex switch on and double teamed BuTay; they earned a GayVN nod for Best Threesome) and *Workin' It Out*, a nod to the infamous *Black Workout* series of the late 80s/early 90s (and, for those in the know, the tawdry *h*enanigans at the New York Sports Club in Harlem), which brought Full Moons seven GayVN nominations: Best Director (EJ), Best Actor (BuTay), Best Duo (BuTay and Tiger Tyson), Best Orgy (BuTay, Castro/Supreme, Shorty J, Jovonnie, Sexcyone, and Sarge), Best Screenplay (Henry "The Head" Howdini and BuTay), Best

Music (gay hip-hop artists Tim'm T. West, Tori Fixx, Bry'Nt, and Shorty Roc), and Best Ethnic-Themed Video (yes, a bone thrown to the "minority" flicks that usually find themselves shut out of the other categories). It only took the last category (the first winner that didn't feature white actors in the cast) but the recognition was a vindication for EJ, who found himself mentioned in the same sentences as powerhouse porn director/moguls Chi Chi LaRue, Michael Lucas, and Bruce Cam, and invited to give insight as an "expert" in the trade publications and at porn conventions. In some quarters, Full Moons was no longer dismissed as just another "urban" (read: Black/Latino/Blatino) studio, a la CoCoBoyz, Latino Fan Club, and StreetLife.

He had the profits, he had the profile, he finally had the respect. But there was still one thing EJ wanted.

"EJ, no." Evan pushed him back. EJ attempted to kiss him. They were alone in the office on this particular night.

EJ leaned forward; they were nose to nose. "Evan, please. I ... I have wanted you for so long."

"I know."

"No, you don't know. It's not about fucking you. It's about making love to you."

Evan recalled their discussion about mixing biz and pleasure. "We work together. We're friends. It would ruin both relationships."

"But I love you."

Evan's eyes widened. "You ... do?"

"Yes, I do. I always have. And I am in love with you."

"You are?"

"Yes."

Uh-oh. Evan could tell by the look in his eyes he was serious. He'd been in this situation before, only he was the one saying those words. So he repeated what had been said to him. "I ... love you too, EJ, but ... not that way."

EJ stepped back, looking down, defeated.

Evan reached out for him. EJ pulled away.

And he continued pulling further away. It was never easy for EJ, watching Evan being fucked by so many others, and it certainly didn't get any easier after disclosing his feelings and being rejected. But now he was *humiliated* and had to continue directing the man he loved and was in love with being fucked by others. Before it was frustrating; now it was painful, and it pained Evan to see the pain he was going through, but what could he do? EJ became indifferent; he soon addressed him only as BuTay, and would only discuss business with him.

Things became surprisingly less tense between them when Evan and Tracy Armond Murrell, aka Kayo, fell in love. EJ "discovered" him, dancing as a go-go boy at Escuelita. He was one of those cornbread-fed boys ("From the 'ham") who ventured to the Big Apple to make it big. Tall, thick and chiseled. Rich brown skin. Doe-eyed. Square jaw. Full lips. A smile brighter than a neon sign.

Yup, one look and he K.O.'s you (EJ gave him the perfect stage name). As the artist once again known as Prince used to sang, *You sex-y mother-fucker.*

When Kayo cruised (he didn't have a bop, strut, or swagger, yet it was just as masculine but much more regal) into the office, and his and BuTay's eyes met ... *WHAM!!!* It was a first sight thing. As they were introduced, they shook hands and neither wanted to let go. As they made small talk on the love seat, Kayo pulled BuTay onto his left thigh; BuTay ran his fingers through his dark brown locs. They rehearsed the kissing scene at least a dozen times—and that was the *only* scene they rehearsed. When the cameras rolled and Kayo placed his arms around BuTay's waist, they *gazed* into each other's eyes and *kissed*. And when BuTay eased his azz down on Kayo's dick and they became *one*, everyone—the cameraman, the grip guy, the lighting director, the script guy, and the fluff boy (whose services weren't needed at all)—could clearly see they were *not* acting. And when they, as Kayo would later describe it, "caught some heaven" ... yes, the earth titled off its axis for a second or two, it was that seismic and powerful. But everyone, including BuTay, was shocked when EJ didn't yell cut. He just let them do their thing. EJ was still lovestruck, but he wasn't stupid. He'd filmed a couple hundred scenes over a decade and had never seen chemistry like it. This wasn't something you could cajole, coerce, or create; it just was. He was witnessing magic; they were a perfect match. He saw the bottom line: the dollar sign.

So, as BuTay and Kayo repeated that love scene at Evan's place later that night, EJ plotted how to exploit their pairing to the fullest. The dynamic duo made four flicks together— *A Love For All Times* (which presented them falling in lust in three different eras—the Harlem Renaissance, the disco years, and the high-top fade nineties); *Fed Sex* (yes, Kayo delivered a package BuTay *loved* receiving); *Same Script, Different Ass* (Kayo does the same scene three times but saves the very best bootay for last); and the #1 fan fave, *Fruit Salad* (in which Kayo ate slices of cantaloupe, orange and pineapple out of BuTay's azz)—and became the new joint face of Full Moons. They were inseparable; you didn't see one without the other. Twenty-four hours after meeting, Tracy packed up his duffel and moved out of the two bedroom apartment in Rego Park, Queens he was sharing with three roommates (he had the futon sofa on odd nights, the carpeted floor on even) and into Evan's two-bedroom co-op in Fort Greene, Brooklyn. Evan stopped ordering from San Cho's Chinese Palace, the corner deli, and Junior's every other day; Tracy whipped up meals that were filling, nutritious, and good. Tracy encouraged Evan to write more; Evan encouraged Tracy to enroll in chef school. They attended Black Gay Prides in New York, Detroit, Philly, Boston, Miami, and Oakland, where they were feted as the new Bobby and Flex-Deon Blake. They vacationed in Hawaii the week of Halloween, spent Thanksgiving with Tracy's grandmother in Birmingham, and visited Evan's cousin and his partner in Charlotte for Christmas. They celebrated New Year's in Times Square, probably the only Black men kissing for close to an hour (with all those stupefyingly drunk people, no one seemed to notice). Tracy threw Evan a surprise birthday party Martin Luther King weekend in Atlanta. They had front row seats for Oleta Adams at B.B. King's Blues Club and Grill on Valentine's Day.

Then Tracy was killed a week later in a hit-and-run accident in Harlem. The driver, who was followed home by another motorist, was cited just one month earlier for driving while intoxicated, his sixth DUI citation in two years. It was because of this history (and the promise from the D.A. that second degree murder charges would be sought) that the driver entered a guilty plea to voluntary vehicular manslaughter and leaving the scene of an accident. He'd eventually be sentenced to twelve years in jail and three years probation.

Evan was *devastated*. He had to identify Tracy at the morgue. He sobbed as the coroner pulled back the sheet revealing Tracy's scarred face and mangled upper body, and didn't stop for an entire day. Then he stayed awake for an entire day, holding and smelling all of Tracy's clothes. Then he slept for an entire day. Then he became angry. And angrier. And *angrier*. Tracy was his first love, his *only* love—he'd never felt that way about anyone. Not only did he never know love like that before, he never knew that kind of love existed. He'd given up hope on finding THE ONE long before he was in the game. He didn't believe in "soul mates"—until Tracy. They fell into each other's eyes, lips, arms, and lives as if they'd always been waiting for the other. And he was only in his life for eleven months. *Eleven months. Fuck* all that "look-on-the-bright-side" bullshit: *You two were lucky to have found the other when you did; Be glad you had what you had and shared what you did; In this business, most people fly solo, and some would kill to experience what you had with him.* Evan *wasn't* thankful for what he had with him because it wasn't enough. They deserved to be together and they deserved more than what they had. The universe couldn't give them a year, *one lousy fucking year?* Instead of being in mourning, Evan was enraged.

EJ wasn't grieving, either. Just a week after Kayo's death, he released a *Best of* compilation that could only be downloaded on-line. The extras included "bloopers" (fumbled lines), "home movies" (clips of Kayo at the office and appearing at different erotica events) and Kayo's audition, in which he rubbed his body down with oil, jerked off and, on a dare, let EJ fuck him with his tongue, then his fingers, then his dick. As too many of Full Moons models were aware, EJ had the very bad habit of slipping a micky in the drink of the newbie. It wouldn't knock them out; just bring down their defenses, so he could "seduce" them into doing things they wouldn't normally do. Kayo claimed to be a total top but given the back he had (plump and protruding) and his six month stint as an escort when he first arrived in New York (his former profile on Rent Boy identified him as "99% top"), the chance that someone *hadn't* been up in it was slim.

EJ was taking credit for being that someone. When one logs on to the Full Moons website, they're greeted with the banner: *Watch Kayo Get Krunked in His Trunk For The First Time!* Evan couldn't believe that EJ could be so tacky and classless, not to mention sneaky: one night many years ago when they were both a little tipsy, EJ disclosed that he had a complex about coming up short in the crotch (one would think hanging around so many Black and Latino men would make that hang-up worse). This explained why Kayo yelped with delight when the ass was tossed and the fingers probed him, but could barely be heard *breathing* while being fucked. And those moans and groans? They were from *other* films he'd done (BuTay would know; he co-starred in them *and* shared a bed with the man). So, Kayo was knocked out from boredom, just didn't feel a thing, or both. To portray himself as a good lover, EJ had to doctor the video's soundtrack (naturally, there are no shots of his dick, just him trying to bump and grind away to no avail, then a rather unimpressive sperm spritz on Kayo's azz).

Evan stormed into the office. "What the hell do you think you're doing?"

EJ was seated at his desk. He didn't look up from what he was reading. "What do you mean?"

"Don't you think it's too soon to put out something like that?"

"No."

"Well, it is."

He looked up on that one. "Don't tell me how to run my business."

"*Your* business? Who do you think helped build this business?"

"*Helped* build. I'm glad you know it."

"The least you could've done is let *me* know. I shouldn't have to find out about it elsewhere."

"You were his boyfriend, not his agent."

"What is your problem?"

"I don't have one."

"Why are you being nasty?"

"I'm not. I'm just being realistic."

"If *that* was the case, you wouldn't have embarassed yourself like that."

"I haven't."

"You don't think so?"

"I know so."

"You obviously haven't been cruising the blogosphere. You're a laughing stock."

"Like I care what they think. They didn't purchase 3,000 copies of the collection in three days. If anything, they are giving me free publicity blogging about it."

"This is not good publicity, EJ. Only a desperate, despicable man would release such crap, *and* put himself in it. You're fooling yourself."

"No, *you* are."

"*Oh?* And what am I fooling myself about?"

"About how you feel."

"About what?"

"You know."

Evan scoffed. "Why are you so fucking bitter?"

"Bitter? About what?"

"About us *not* being an us."

"Don't flatter yourself, BuTay."

"My *name* is *Evan*."

"*My* name suits you best. And you've proven me right by showing the world that what you sit on—and *who* you sit on— makes it your most appealing attribute."

"*Fuck you, EJ.*"

"You had your chance. Now, please leave, I have work to do. And make sure you're here tomorrow morning at six."

"What? What the hell for?"

"Because someone has to fill in for your boyfriend on the shoot."

Evan heaved. "First, I am just getting back from Birmingham—"

"Yet you had the energy to come over and berate me ... ?"

"*Secondly*, I am not ready to go back to work."

"You have no choice."

"Say what?"

"You are still under contract. You don't get to choose what films you do; *I* make that decision." He smiled. "Besides, I'm sure he'd want you to carry on for him."

Evan was flabbergasted. "You said I could have the rest of the month off."

"Six a.m. Sharp. Please." He turned back to the paperwork.

Evan went home and read his contract, and there it was in black and white: Clause 23/a did in fact say that EJ had that right and if BuTay didn't follow his orders, he could be sued for breach of contract and any monies owed him by the studio would be used to not only pay other actors for the work he won't do but EJ's legal fees. EJ never had a reason to invoke that clause before; even when they weren't getting along, he always put the image and reputation of Full Moons way above being spiteful. Not any longer.

BuTay arrived at the office at 5:59am.

He was contractually bound to do three more films after filling in for Kayo in *Hot Sauce* (it wasn't used as a condiment). He was slammed by Lil' Walter, who was no more than five feet but had one humongous stick. But BuTay's heart wasn't in it. Neither was his ass. But he still gave it "that old college try" (one of EJ's standard lines when he wasn't getting what he wanted out of an actor) and came through—and *came*.

He managed to cum on the next film—*Fat Is Where It's At*—despite being paired with gentlemen who could moonlight as sumo wrestlers. EJ took great glee in watching BuTay being crushed into the mattress by the Latino, and getting thrown around as if he were a rag doll by the white one. The brother was also a blob, but at least he was very agile and had good coordination for a man his size.

And he even came during *Gangstas & Goths*, EJ's disastrous rip-off of *Ruffnecks & Rednecks*—but it wasn't easy. During the entire shoot, he was mentally saying the Lord's Prayer, calling on the angels to protect him from any unholy spirits that surrounded his partner, who looked like one of the devil's disciples: skin white as milk decorated with black eyeliner and black lipstick; black Doc Martens, black stonewashed jeans, black mock, and a black cape; and wavy black hair styled in the shape of horns. That's right, *horns*. It was the tongue piercing that saved the day (he also had them in his chin, both lips, both nostrils, both ears, both eyebrows, and his navel). BuTay had never been kissed with or tasted by a man with one—and it turned him *on*. And Damien (his *given* name; BuTay just knew he'd find 666 engraved on him somewhere) enjoyed eating ass more than fucking it—he spent ten minutes doing the former rather splendidly, fifteen on the latter with very lackluster results, then returned to the former for another twenty thrilling minutes. Since BuTay was lying on his belly, he didn't have to look at Damien's frightening face. They sprung their fountains at the same time.

But BuTay wouldn't be cuming today. EJ was hell bent on sticking it to him one more time. Not showing any compassion or sorrow over Kayo's death nor sympathy for BuTay's loss. Placing him in projects he knew would fuck with or over him. Now, this. His final chance to humiliate BuTay. And once again, someone else would be doing the dirty work. BuTay didn't like his own sperm being on his body and only tolerated it being dumped on his back or butt or legs or ass or chest by others (it's expected in the porn trade). But this ... *this* was just a half-step away from pissing in somebody's face.

Big hunched up. He huffed. He hollered *"I'm cumin', yo"* seven or eight times. (*Then cum already, mother-fucker.*) He aimed. He fired. He fell.

BuTay had pushed him off—and that was no easy feat. Big was a hulky dude, but BuTay managed to unpin his left leg.

As his dick continued to ejaculate onto the floor, Big looked up, incredulous. *"What the fuck, yo?"*

BuTay didn't answer. He just slid off the bed, swooped up his clothes, and barreled down the bunker steps, everyone watching in shock.

EJ was right behind him. He grabbed BuTay's left arm. "Where do you think you're going?"

BuTay snatched it away. *"Get* your fuckin' hands off me."

"You are not going to fuck this up for me."

"Hmph, I just did." He began putting on his clothes.

"You better get your black ass back up there."

"Oh. My *Black* ass? Careful, the red is starting to show on your neck."

"Don't try that race card crap with me."

"You're the one holding—and *dealing*—from that deck."

"I've just about had it with you."

"Oh? And what are you going to do *with* me, Massa?"

"I'm not your Massa. But you have been pimping yourself out as a slave to masters for some time."

"What ever."

"What's the line you use? 'It's my job.' You've been using porn as an excuse to fulfill your desire of being posessed by us. But let a white man who doesn't want to fuck you on camera or pay you for it express genuine interest, and you run in the other direction ... "

"Who the fuck are you, Dr. Frances Cress Welsing? You just can't let it go, can you? I don't want your ass. I *never* wanted your ass. And why *would* I want your ass? But if a Negro *doesn't* want your ass, something's *got* to be wrong with him, right? And you don't think you're suffering from post traumatic slave master syndrome?"

He pointed his finger at BuTay's chest. "I expect you to fulfill your contractual obligations."

"I already have."

"I don't know what makes you think you're so special. We all have to do things in this life we may not want to."

"I do not like my face being used as a toilet. But then, you already knew that."

"Either you get back up there or I will haul your ass into court."

"For what? Refusing to be assaulted by sperm?"

"And I'll let the IRS know about your under-the-table gigs."

"Let's not go there. You forget, I managed this bitch for a year. Who do you think I learned the shit from? They'll be making a deal with *me* to get to *you*."

EJ was stung but not stuck. He grinned. "*And*, I'll make sure your mother and father receive a collection of your greatest hits on DVD."

Blackmail? How appropriate. But BuTay couldn't be worried about it, and he wasn't. He was tired. Tired of fighting. Tired of feeling helpless. Tired of feeling alone. Tired of feeling lonely. He was disgusted with the whole thing, and disgusted with himself. He wanted his man back. He wanted his body back; it hadn't belonged to him in years, and he'd lost a piece of himself every time he gave someone a piece. He wanted to be able to tell his parents what he did for a living ("public relations" has been the usual line—and it's not altogether untrue). He wanted to write that Great American Novel, which he hadn't written a single line for since becoming an actor. He wanted his life back. And if freedom meant his being a videho' would come to light, bring it.

Of course, he couldn't let EJ think that would scare him. So he hit him *way* below the belt. "Secret? You mean, like having a four-inch dick and drugging others so you can get your pebble off?"

EJ *fumed*; the red was really showing on his neck now. *"You stupid nigger!"*

There was a unified, audible gasp from the gallery upstairs. BuTay thought: *Was this lily-white crew genuinely shocked that he had called me such a vulgar name—or were they genuinely shocked that he had called me such a vulgar name to my face?* BuTay knew the epithet—or something like it—would spew from his mouth sooner or later. It may no longer be fashionable or acceptable for white folks to just come right out and call a Black person a nigger, but that doesn't mean they've stopped. Some forget that it is the 21st century and let it rip (like Michael "Fifty years ago we'd have you upside down with a fucking fork up your ass" Richards). But most dance around it (i.e., "that Muslim, Kenyan, Socialist, Fake-Birth-Certificate-Having President"). And it always comes down to you not knowing your place. It wasn't until he had the gall to reject a white man's advances or challenge their paternalistic, colonialitsic attitude that buying his time meant that they were buying *him* that BuTay went from being lovely, gorgeous, alluring, a dream/fantasy come true and all that to porch monkey, darkie, mud boy, jigaboo, Magilla Gorilla, and the Big N.

BuTay knew where it came from, that it demonstrated just how much contempt they had for Black men (if not all Black people), and that he was and would have to be the bigger person and ignore their ignorance. EJ was no different. *He* may have thought he was a different kind of white man (don't they all think that?), but he was still white. Once again, BuTay would have to rise above it and rise above him. But this time, because he *knew* the white man ... he really wanted to haul off and punch the shit out of him.

But Big beat him to it.

Wrapped in a white towel, Big happened to be standing just a few feet behind EJ. He snatched EJ by the back of his collar, swung him around, and bopped him in the left cheek. EJ flew over what used to be Evan's desk and into the file cabinet.

Paralyzed with fascination (or was it fear?), the crew just stood in silence, mouths agape.

"Who you callin' nigger, *cracker?*" Big bellowed at EJ, who was knocked the fuck out. He turned to BuTay. "Man, ya shoulda told me that ain't yo' thang. This mo'-fo' said you like gettin' shot in the face. No foul. You cool?"

Hmm ... as many times EJ hoped to lay my ass out behind that desk ...

BuTay smiled at Big. "Yeah. I am now."

HOW STANLEY GOT HIS BACK IN GROOVE

"So ... " I began. "I have an announcement to make."

I was at Giorgio's, a gourmet coffee shop on Christopher Street in Greenwich Village, having Tuesday evening tea with my best friends, Ulester "Les" Nevins and Marq Malone. Well, we don't drink tea but *spill* the tea over a bottle of wine and a small turtle cheesecake, one of the most popular items sold by Marq's catering business, Sweet Treats. Giorgio's has an exclusive deal as the only dessert spot in the area to serve his prize-winning cakes and cookies (which meant our check was on the house).

Les perked up. "You're joining a gym!" Les visits David Barton five days a week and has been trying to get me to go for years.

"Now, you know that ain't it," Marq argued; he, like me, is proud of his love handles. "You're going back to school to finish your degree ... ?"

Hmph, I'd have to finish a *semester* first. In the fall of 1989, I did two months at Baruch College (where I met both Marq and Les) and never went back after mid-terms. "No."

Les took another guess. "You're quitting your job—*again.*"

Now, *that* usually was the case. I've never held one longer than two years. You'd think the economic downturn would've put the brakes on this habit but it hasn't: the average time I've gone without a job (three weeks) hasn't changed. I'm currently working on month twenty two as a Transportation Security Administration officer at JFK. "No."

Of course, they were both surprised to hear that. Marq sat back and contemplated, while Les tapped his wine glass with the diamond stud he wore on his right index finger.

"*I've got it!*" shouted Les, startling the Filipino bus boy, who almost dropped the tray of dishes he was carrying. "You're *finally* going to stop fucking *yourself!*"

The bus boy stared at me, flabbergasted.

I frowned. "You don't have to broadcast it to the world."

"Given how much fuckin' you did *before* your vow of celibacy, the world is well aware that you've been on hiatus."

Indeed. I'd gotten such a … *reputation,* that sailors continue to blow up my cell and ring my buzzer during Fleet Week, having received word *way* out on the high seas about the skillz of Supa Dupa Head (Karrine Steffans, who?) and His Supa Dupa Bunz. Unfortunately for them, by my thirtieth birthday I'd spent half my life fucking—and I was sick of it. *Literally* sick of it. Just *thinking* of doing it made me physically ill. The joy, the excitement, the chills … all gone. Marq knew the reason why: "It's easy when you're easy." And I *was* easy—*too* easy. And it was certainly easy *to* be easy: Men—regardless of stage, situation, or sexual orientation—are built for it, socialized for it, some might even say wired for it. Sex had become not just my favorite contact sport but the only way I interacted with other men (except Marq and Les). So Marq suggested I cleanse myself by abstaining for six months (Les didn't believe I'd last six *hours*). Yet even he was amazed when that six months bloomed into six years. But my body *and* my mind really needed the break.

"I still don't see how you've been able to go nine years, nine months, three weeks, and six days without it," Les continued.

I stared at him in disbelief.

Marq was also floored that Les had the exact length of time down. "You have been keeping tabs on another man's sexless life? *That* is scary."

"I haven't exactly been sexless," I defended.

Marq knew exactly who ... well, *what* I was referring to. "Please, Big Ben does not count." *Big Ben* being my rather handy, dandy, nine-inch dildo ...

"Of course he does—in a way," argued Les. "He's probably the most reliable, efficient man you've ever been fucked by."

Since Big Ben's always been there whenever, wherever, and however I needed him, he was. But it was a rather embarrassing, depressing assessment: my longest and most fulfilling (sexual) relationship has been with a battery-powered device.

"So, who's the lucky guy?" Marq asked.

"I don't know yet." I turned to Les; I knew he had a *very* long list of potentials he could dial up in seconds. "And I'm in no rush to do it. If it's in a month, so be it."

Les sucked his teeth. "*A month?* Uh, it is summer time in New York *fuckin'* City ... "

"Actually, summer doesn't officially start until next Tuesday," Marq corrected him.

"Thank you, Sam Champion," Les snapped back. "The calendar may not know it, but Mother Nature sure does. Anyway, there is no way you will be able to hold out for an entire month with all the candy roaming these streets. Hell, it could happen in the next hour."

Marq pointed toward the entrance. "Or the next minute."

I caught the tall, torn speci-man in the window, walking by in slow motion.

"That's the *third* time he's passed," Marq revealed. "And each time, his eyes have been fixed on *you*."

And, as he walked back up the block, he passed the window again, his head twisting further to the right and not letting me out of his crosshairs.

"*Damn.* Junior likes what he sees," observed Les. "And he plans on telling you himself."

The stranger entered the eatery and headed straight for our table. He wore a pair of stonewashed light blue jeans, a wife beater that hugged the hell out of his v-shaped torso and ten-pack (yes, I counted the rips), and brown open toe sandals. Small gold hoops were in his right ear and left nostril. The hazel eyes sparkled, the brows were bushy, and the lips pouty and pretty. He rocked a dark brown afro, a la Maxwell from back in the day.

He smiled; there was a dimple in his left cheek. "Pardon me, gents. Don't mean to interrupt ... "

Sitting just a couple of feet away from the stranger, Les leaned forward, focusing on the young man's very visible bulge. "No problem. *You* are a *welcome* interruption."

Marq cleared his throat. "Heel, Fang."

The stranger giggled like a little boy—and, given that he was over six feet, that was something to see. He turned to me. "Mr. Brewster?"

"Uh, yes?"

"*Stanley* Brewster?"

"Yyyyes?"

He punched the air; was that his way of jumping for joy? "Wow, I can't believe this. I thought I'd never see you again."

"Do I know you?"

"Oh, I'm sorry. The last time you saw me I was ten years old."

Sipping on his wine, Marq coughed.

"My name is Robert Carpenter. Bobby for short. I was in your fifth grade phys ed class."

I had to rewind the mind. *He couldn't mean* ... "At Knowledge Hall in Fort Greene?"

"Yup."

"You're kidding?"

"Nope. It's OK if you don't remember me. I *have* grown a lot since then."

"And in all the right places," Les mumbled.

"I'm sorry, I don't remember you. That period is ... a blur." And it was. Just five hours after the school's athletics assistant resigned, the academic dean offered me the position after he had me (according to him, I had the right *flex* for the job). I had just quit working at a UPS call center (I lasted there twenty months) and he needed someone to fill in for the remainder of the school year, which amounted to four months. I only assisted with one class; most of my time was spent performing clerical duties (and avoiding being pinched and groped by him). So I was curious ... "How could you remember me from all those years ago?"

"How could I not, with you running and tumbling from one end of the gym to the other, in those clingy, thermal, dark grey shorts?"

Those clingy, thermal, dark grey shorts (which I still happen to own) have always turned the heads of men *and* women. Was he making fun of me?

He made it clear he wasn't. "In case you didn't realize, that was a compliment."

I was actually blushing—but should I be? He just admitted that, as a (barely) pre-teen, he was hot for teacher. I had to change the subject. "Uh, these are my best friends, Marq and Les."

Bobby shook both their hands. "Nice to meet you, gents."

"You, too," Marq acknowledged.

Les rested his elbow on the table and propped his right palm under his chin. He was the Don Lemon of our trio. "So, *Bobby*, I'm sure you're no longer in elementary school."

Bobby chuckled. "I just finished my junior year at Howard."

"Ah. Majoring in?"

"Music production and management."

"So, you're ... 20?"

"Yup. Will be 21 in November."

Les looked at me. "And, you're home for the summer?"

"I am."

Les raised his glass in my direction, passing the baton to me.

But Bobby snatched it up and ran with it first. "Mr. Brewster ... "

"Please, call me Stanley."

"Thank you. Stanley ... this will sound ... odd, but ... I'd really like to take you out."

"Take me out?"

"Yeah."

"Where?"

"On a date."

"You ... would?"

"Yeah."

"Why?"

"Why not?"

My eyes darted from Les to Marq, then back to Bobby. "When?"

"How 'bout this Saturday?"

"Take down my number."

He plugged it into his iPhone. My ancient LG flip, which was on the table, buzzed.

"And now you've got me," he winked.

I saw his number flash on the screen. "That I do."

"I'll give you a shout on Friday."

"OK."

"So glad I ran into you." He extended his hand.

I accepted it; the boy had a *grip*. "I am, too."

We slowly released the other.

"Try not to talk about me too much after I leave," he directed at all three of us.

"Oh, your ears are gonna be on *fire*," Les promised him.

Bobby giggled, again; he was *so* cute when he did. "You all have a good night."

"You, too," Les and I responded. Marq just nodded.

Both Les and I *inhaled* when we got a gander at the buffet Bobby had in the back.

Bobby exited, waving to me as he passed by the window.

Les grabbed the specialty drink menu card on the table and began fanning himself; some of the air found its way to me (and *I* needed it, too). "Now, *that* is something the Lord made," he testified. "No wonder He had to rest on the seventh day. And, he is something the Lord *sent*. Talk about divine intervention."

Marq filled our empty glasses. "I'm pretty sure God has more important things to be concerned with than our best friend's carnal conquests."

"Hell, even *He* knows it's time Stan got his back in groove—and Bobby certainly wants to help him do just that."

"Uh-huh, and then *Stan's* gonna end up on somebody's registry as a sex offender. He's twice his age. He was f-u-c-k-i-n' before Bobby was a-b-c-in'." Marq was so proper he would only spell out curse words.

"So what? The man may not be old enough to drink but he's certainly old enough to crick."

"Crick?"

"Yeah, I heard one of these young'uns use it the other day. And they were *not* talking about a knot you get in your neck."

Tired of being talked about, I jumped in. "Bobby asked me out on a *date*; we'll see where it goes."

Les sipped his wine. "We know *where* it's gonna go. And *I* can't wait to hear all the lewd, lascivious, lusty details."

I began thinking of all the very lewd, lascivious, and lusty things I wanted to do to him, that I wanted him to do to me, and that I wanted us to do together. I got the shivers and felt a familiar sensation in the rump.

I downed my glass of wine. I raised my left hand to get the waiter's attention. "Excuse me? We'll need another bottle."

Bobby called me at noon on Friday with the plan: meet him at BBQ in the East Village at six for dinner. Since he was a student, I didn't expect him to treat me to a five-star restaurant ... but *BBQ?* I never cared for the space (way too cramped), the clientele (too many folks with too little table manners), the food (the most bland, flavorless roasted chicken on the planet) or the service (too much attitude from and not enough attention paid by the staff). However, I was most willing to make the sacrifice; I'd just have to suck it up so that I could ... suck *him* up later on.

It was still early so it wasn't that crowded. I settled on the turkey burger, which wasn't bad. Bobby had a rib and chicken combo, which he devoured in fifteen minutes. The waitress was so enamored with Bobby that she charged him for one large margarita instead of two.

After he took care of the check (refusing to let me pay the tip), he revealed that we'd be going to the theater.

Of course, I responded with: "A musical or play?"

"Musical."

"What's it called?"

"*You'll* see."

The first surprise was *where* the performance was taking place: the Lesbian and Gay Community Center. I hadn't visited since the renovations began in the late nineties. The show was being performed in the main hall on the third floor.

Then I saw the poster: seven nude men with the show's title emblazoned across their private areas.

"*Nekked Boiz Sangin'*!?" I had to say it out loud.

Bobby just nodded and smiled.

The show was an obvious rip-off of the hugely popular and mostly-white *Naked Boys Singing!* Of course, this cast was all-Black—except for one Puerto Rican. All different hues, heights, and hefts, each man, ranging in age from early twenties to mid-forties, was stacked and sinfully sexy. They faced the audience with their crotches covered by their hands, church fans, or a tambourine (even so, some were having a *very* hard time concealing and containing their packages). There were no sets and very little choreography (most of the bouncing and bopping coming during the "Bootylicious like Beyonce" number).

After the cast took their bows to thunderous applause, whistles and catcalls (there were about two hundred people in attendance, a diverse mix in ethnicity, nationality, gender, and age), Corey Corey—the tallest Nekked Boi, who sported a cherry Mohawk-like 'do—stepped forward. "Thank you all. We would like to take this opportunity to acknowledge our Producer, who is in the house tonight, for making this all possible: Robert Carpenter, Jr."

Bobby stood up and saluted the cast, as if he were their drill sergeant. I was so shell-shocked about the show's name that I just glanced over the program. I took a second look and there he was: Robert Carpenter, Jr. the Producer was Bobby Carpenter my date.

As Bobby spoke with the manager of the Center, I watched the actors sign autographs and take pics (in their underwear) with some very ebullient audience members (one gent had the entire cast hold him up against their waists; another, above their heads).

"Were you expecting *Hair* or *The Book of Mormon?*" Bobby inquired as we left the Center.

"No. But this was still quite the surprise. Why didn't you tell me we were going to see a show you produced?"

"I wanted to see your honest reaction to it. What did you think?"

"Well ... " *OK, how do I put this ...* "I enjoyed it very much."

"No you didn't."

"I did too."

"Come on, you can be honest."

"I ... can?"

"Yeah."

"Well ... it stinks."

"I know."

"*But*, it was fun to watch."

"And that's why I produced it. The crowd didn't go wild because of the score, or the story, or the acting; they went wild because it's nekked boiz sangin'. And *they* live up to the title. They could be up there doing their ABC's and the audience would be all in."

"Actually, their doing their ABC's *would* improve the show. How did you come to produce it?"

"I went to high school with the brutha who wrote it. He's a theater major at NYU."

"How did you raise the money to do it?"

"My aunt threw a cocktail investor party at her home last October. She's a lawyer and reps other Black gays and lesbians with deep pockets. After presenting the proposal and production schedule, and previewing a few of the songs, they wrote me checks on the spot."

Those few songs *must've* been the only memorable ones in the show: the title song (which is also the opening number), "Birthday Suit," and the finale, "Get Nekked With Us." If I was at that party, I might've written a check, too. "You're a good salesman," I complimented.

"Thanks. If you want folks to come out of their pockets in *this* economy, you gotta be."

"But I thought your goal was to manage musical artists?"

"It is. And I am. But a manager has to be a man—or woman—of all mediums. Whatever's gonna make me and my clients green, I'm in that scene."

"Is the Manuel Gonzalez in the show the same one you were telling me about during dinner?"

"Yup."

"He's really got some pipes on him."

"I know. He's gonna be another Tevin Campbell."

Tevin Campbell? There's a name I hadn't heard since ... the twentieth century. Manuel's voice did in fact favor his. But Bobby wasn't even *alive* when Tevin hit the scene. I guess I expected him to throw out a name like Usher, Mario, or Chris Brown.

My quizzical look gave me away. He grinned. "What *you* know about him?"

"I was about to ask *you* the same question." I smiled. "Hmm ... this means you get a cut as a producer *and* as his manager. I believe they call that double dippin'."

"I'm an expert in that area." He winked.

"Aren't you afraid of being sued for copyright infringement?"

"Nah. We say it is inspired by the original. Besides, it's so small-scale and bare bones, we aren't a threat. And how would they look coming after us? That'd just give us more press—and sell more tickets."

"Are you afraid to have such a ... stinker on your resume?"

"Everybody's gotta start somewhere. And not everything one does in their career is going to be the creme de la creme. Besides, the show is packin' them in and is already in the black. What was supposed to be a two weekend engagement has turned into six. And we've got the eye of a few off-Broadway houses. That's the only thing future investors will be looking at, not the reviews."

We stopped at a red light.

"So, was taking me to see the show your way of saying you want to get *me* nekked?" I chuckled.

He shifted behind me, placing his right hand on the street pole a few inches above my head. "I already said that on Tuesday when I mentioned them thermal grey shorts." His voice had a little more rumble to it.

"I still don't see how you could be checking out the teacher's aide at that age."

"Ha, you made it easy. I was glad Mr. Huckleberry quit. With you in the class, it finally got interesting—especially when you would warm-up with us." His eyes darted down. "Watching you jingle. Watching *all* of you jingle. Oh, my damn. Gave me serious wet dreams."

"For real?"

"For realz. And they started again Tuesday night."

"They did?"

"Yup. But now ... I don't plan on just dreamin' about you."

And right there, on the southeast corner of 8th Avenue and 14th Street, he gave me *that* look—and I gave it right back. It was *like* a kiss, the prelude to the kiss.

It was *on.*

Bobby knew what to do: He stepped into the street and, miracle of miracles for a Black man (especially going uptown on a Saturday night), hailed a cab like that. We climbed in. I gave the driver my address. As he zoomed up to my place in Harlem, we sat close, in silence, holding hands, my right arm resting on his left thigh. In twenty minutes, we were in my apartment.

And twenty minutes after that, Bobby was in me.

I expected Bobby to ... well, get me *crinked*, and he didn't disappoint (I kept hearing Madea testify *"Ha-lay-loo-yer!"* as he held onto my handles and rode all up in what he affectionately dubbed my "Promised Land"). But I *didn't* expect him to be so ... *thorough.* After all, I was his age once; at 20, I humped just about anything with a pulse and there wasn't a science to it (or so I thought). For most young'uns, the energy level is sky high but the stamina is super low. They may have the right size tool but don't know how to harness its power. They may have the mechanics down but employ very little technique. They're all about gettin' a nutt—they don't know how to crack one.

So I figured he'd pounce, then bounce on that first night. And I would've been alright with that. He was just my type and would give me that jump start, putting me back in the game and prepping me for whomever and whatever would cum my way the rest of the summer and beyond.

Yeah, he *fooled* me.

I never knew what ... *ecstasy* was until Bobby laid his fingers, his mouth, his tongue, his teeth, even his nostrils on me.

It was as if I was being *touched* by another man for the very first time. He wasn't fuckin' me; he was—dare I say it?—*lovin'* me. Lovin' me like a grown man. Like a grown-*ass* man.

And then, of course, there was the Dick. Yes, with a capital D.

Oh. That. Dick.

It knocked on my (back) door, came on in, stretched, stretched *out*, and made itself right at home. Bobby got up in it and ...

It. Was. A. Wrap.

Which is why I nicknamed Bobby "The Boy with the *Ooo La La La*," since all I could coo when he was tearin' it up was *"Ooo la la la."* Yup, like Lady T. *It's the way that you feel when you know it's real.* When the sex has been this damn good, I've been known to holler to the heavens at such high decibels that the cops were called on one occasion for allegedly breaking the city's "quality of life" noise ordinance.

But Bobby made me scream—*inside.* A quiet storm will do that to you.

And did he know how to double dip! *Mph!*

I *had* to have it. Every day. Hell, sometimes twice a day. Like the Boss, once in the morning, once in the evening.

And *Bobby* had to have it, too. Every day. Sometimes twice a day. AM, PM. Just like Miss Ross. And he gave it up the same way he gave it—without reservation or apology. Nothin' could be finer than seeing in my bureau mirror: the backs of his lovely thighs hugging my chest, his lovely legs draped over my shoulders, and his lovely toes pointed straight toward the ceiling as he pleaded with school-boy innocence, *"Give it to me, Mista B, yeah ... "*

You want it, you got it.

He (well, we) got a kinky kick out of me wearing my TSA uniform and pulling him out of the security line to do some ... *extra* screening.

After the routine pat down—allowing my hands to linger longer than the law allows in each area (arms, biceps, chest, abs, back, butt, thighs, calves)—I settled on the spot that seemed to have a mind of its own: his crotch. I eyed it with suspicion. "Sir, are you carrying any contraband on your person?"

"No."

I pushed down on it with my palm. "Are you in possession of any materials banned by the FAA?"

"No."

"Well, I'm going to have to inspect this area further—or would you rather go through the x-ray machine?"

"Inspect away!"

I reached inside his jeans and groped the goods. "Sir, what's *this?*"

He grabbed *my* goods. "What's *that?*"

"Sir, do you know that it is a federal offense to physically assault a TSA employee?"

"Well, what if I wanna be physically assaulted *by* the TSA employee?"

He got his wish. I ordered him to strip nekked and bend over for some extra, *extra* screening. None of the maneuvers I performed on *and* in him could be found in the TSA customer service manual.

But he got even when I wore that pair of clingy, thermal, dark grey shorts he loved so much.

"Mr. Brewster, can you show me how to do a proper hand stand?" he squealed as if he were ten years old.

I knew what he was up to and was more than willing to play along. "Sure, Bobby."

I demonstrated (and was surprised that I could still do one). As soon as I was in a stationary position, he kneeled down in front of me. "I bet you've never been sucked—*or* fucked—upside down."

He didn't give me a chance to respond. He pulled up and took off my shorts. By the time he got to double-dippin', my shoulders replaced my hands so that I could jerk as he jacked me the fuck up (well, *down*).

Of course, we didn't *need* to create scenarios. Seemed we couldn't do *anything* without it leading to ... you know.

Like, when we were sitting up in bed one morning, reading the Sunday paper.

He took off his reading glasses (they had a thick, rectangular, turquoise frame, which made him look *so* adorkable). "I'm gonna get some juice, you want some?"

"No. But can you bring me a slice of watermelon?"

"Sure."

He returned a few minutes later. "You want it now or later?"

I looked up. "I want it ... "

There he stood with a slice of watermelon—and his dick through the center.

Needless to say, my sheets got very sticky—and so did we.

There's also the time I corn rowed his hair. Of course, I had to wash it first. What did he do? He came into the kitchen—nekked.

"Put some clothes on," I instructed.

"Why?"

"Because I'm washing your *hair*, not your body."

"I don't want my shirt to get wet."

"And what about *below* the waist?"

"Like you ain't never seen it all before. What, you can't control yourself being so close to me?" He winked. He assumed the position: hunched over, ass sticking out.

I controlled myself. But then he began running his ass into my dick as I switched sides to condition, then shampoo.

"Stop doing that."

"Doing what?"

I smacked him on both cheeks with my right hand. "You know damn well what."

There goes that little boy giggle.

After rinsing him for the final time, he grabbed the towel on the counter and began drying his hair. This, of course, made his ass jiggle. And with those cheeks a-clappin' and those missed trails of water streaking down his back and disappearing into that coin slot ... my tongue had to follow.

"Oh, my damn," he moaned.

Oh, my damn is right. That is some sweet, smokin' hot, honey brown sugar mol*ass*es.

Before you knew it he was bent *all* the way forward, folded in and holding *me* by the ankles, as I pounded and pounded and *pounded*, knocking the rest of the wetness out of his hair and all over the floor.

Then there was the evening we had a double feature. We watched my pick first: *The Devil Wears Prada*. He hadn't seen it. He enjoyed it.

I was not pleased with his choice. *"Willy Wonka?"*

"Yeah, *Willy Wonka*."

"Why do you want to watch this?"

"It's got a great score. Gene Wilder is hella funny. And I love it when all those kids get theirs in the end for being greedy and sneaky."

He watched the movie. I watched him. And the more excited he got watching it, the more excited I got watching him.

I leaned on him, in *that* way. "Willy. Wonka."

He glanced at me. He chuckled.

My tongue darted in his left ear. *"Willy,"* I whispered in it.

He squirmed.

I pulled on his dick, which was about to bust out of his Green Hornet shorts. *"Wonk-a."*

"What you doin'?"

"What it *feel* like I'm doin'?"

"See, you ain't fair. I watched your movie without ... "

I tongued the ear and pulled on the dick again.

" ... *interruptions,"* he finished, shivering.

"Well, my chocolate factory is a whole lot better than Willy's."

"Yeah?"

"Yeah."

He peeped and grabbed a handful of my ass. "Well, I *loves* me some chocolate."

"You think you can handle that sugar shack in the back?"

"*That* and then some."

By the time Charlie discovered his Golden Ticket, Bobby was spreading his jizzy frosting on my cupcakes.

All this sexin' left little time for anything (or anyone) else; it's a wonder I had the energy to go to work. So, when Bobby took a weekend trip with his father to see his great grandmother in Atlanta, I paid Les a visit at his co-op in SoHo.

"So, how is Bobby, your new hobby?" Les and I were in his kitchen, he chopping up broccoli and carrots he planned to steam.

All I could do was giggle.

"That good, huh? You've certainly been making up for the last nine plus years. You've skipped our last three Teas."

"I'm sorry."

"*And* you missed Kwesi & Miguel's annual 4th of July bash."

"How was it?"

"Very festive."

"Did you meet anyone?"

"Of course. But no one who is on the radar—yet. I do have both hands full at the moment."

"Ah. And, is one of those handfuls here ... ?"

"He'll be out shortly."

Just then, a brawny white man emerged from the bedroom, wearing just a fire engine red speedo.

He took Les's right hand and kissed it. "Hello, my sexy," he expressed in a very thick Italian accent.

"Gianluigi, this is Stanley, my other best friend."

"Nice to meet you, Gianluigi." I extended my hand to shake his.

"No, no. Beauty such as yours, must be addressed, adorned. Properly." He took my hand and also kissed it.

I smiled. "Thank you."

Les peered at Gianluigi, his eyebrows raised. "You're such a flirt."

"So sorry."

"No you're not. But you will be later on." Les whacked him on his bubble butt.

Gianluigi laughed. "I take shower now. Pardon me, Stanley."

"Of course."

We watched him—well, his ass—as he scurried out.

"*Where* did you find *him*?"

"He's another K & G client." K & G, or Kipper & Graham, is one of the top modeling agencies in the world. If one of their charges is a little too pale, the staff sends him or her over to Les, who owns and operates Sun Kiss, a tanning salon just a few doors down from K & G on Fifth Avenue near Rockefeller Center. It's one of three locations he has in the city (the others are on the Upper East Side and three blocks from his home).

"That tan looks natural," I observed. Gianluigi was definitely a dark Italian: the olive oil skin, the thick lips, the broad nose, the cropped curly black hair, the lightly-dusted hairy forearms, chest and legs.

"It *is* natural. He's straight from the motherland—the island of Sardinia, to be exact—not some garden variety Guido from Bensonhurst or a *Jersey Shore* reject. I met him when I was at their office two weeks ago, signing another contract and picking up fall's deposit."

"And is *he* fall's deposit?"

"He definitely has the potential to be." Every season Les has a new steady, but he's always planning ahead. And he lives up to his initials—going down his roster of lovers is like roll call at the United Nations. He's freaked a Greek, been naughty with a Saudi, and banged an Iraqi in the cracky. One year he collected the Charlies: Suarez from Spain, Halat from Yugoslavia, Tran from Vietnam, and Higginbotham from Barbados. The current top man (figuratively speaking) is Yani Kemal, a Turkish real estate developer who is a dead ringer for Naveen Andrews but speaks like Sir Anthony Hopkins (he's spent his adult years in Liverpool).

"Where is Yani?"

"In Istanbul. He'll be back Monday morning."

"And what will happen with Gianluigi then?"

"He'll be heading to Paris on Sunday to do a showcase for Gucci."

"Mmm. It couldn't have worked out better if ... "

"You *always* gotta plan. Shit just don't happen because you want it to. Which brings me back to Bobby the Hobby. School will be starting for him soon. Have you thought about how you're going to end this?"

"Why would I have to think about that? It's just a summer fling. It will end when the summer does."

"Do you plan on telling him that?"

"Why would I have to say it? It's obvious. It's understood."

"That's what Michael Douglas thought in *Fatal Attraction*."

"Funny."

"It's *not* funny. He has a crush on you. For half his life, the boy has kept a fire burning for you. If you think you two can just end it by walking away ... think again."

I didn't give much thought to Les's warning until the weekend of the Harlem Book Fair. That Saturday was, as Mother Sister (aka Ruby Dee in *Do The Right Thing*) correctly surmised, "hot as the devil," a record-breaking 101 degrees (and it felt like 110). It was also the third straight day in the triple digits and after trekking to JFK in all that Sahara Desert heat (waiting underground for the train being the absolute worst part) the very *last* thing I wanted to do on my day off was wade through the crowds on 135th Street (even if the event was just four blocks away from my apartment). But Bobby wanted to meet Mitchell Crawford, a former creative writing teacher at Knowledge Hall who would be moderating a panel called "From Journalist to Novelist." I didn't know Mitchell worked at KH but I had read and enjoyed both of his books, *You, Me & He* and *You Can't Always Want What You Get*.

After the discussion, Bobby got his own copies autographed and took pictures with Mitchell and his spouse, Raheim Rivers. The look of joy on his face as I snapped them ...

As we walked back to my place, he decided to go down *that* road.

"Man, ain't they something?"

"Who?"

"Mitchell and Raheim. They got it all. Great careers. Two kids. And each other. I read in an article that they plan their work schedules around each other. Raheim even goes on his book tours with him. That's what you call standin' by your man. You want something like that?"

Uh-oh. This is *not* the kind of conversation one should be having with a fuck buddy—surely, he meant "You want something like that *with me?*"—so I put on my Rose Nyland dunce cap. "Something like what?"

"Something like what they have."

"I ... don't know." You'd think I *would* know: I've never been in a relationship yet had plenty of time to consider it during my hiatus. I've just never seen myself being with another man longer than the time it took for us to, you know. Bobby's question was a sign he wanted to unpack our histories and it was my cue to ask, "What about you?"—but I knew better.

It didn't matter, though, because he volunteered an answer to that unspoken question. "I do."

I pretended not to hear him.

Then a few days later, a mid-summer's nightmare occurred: I caught a cold. Not just any cold, but a bug that was traveling along the east coast. Three other TSA security officers on my line were also out for the count.

I couldn't believe it. I don't get sick. The last time I had so much as a sniffle I was twelve years old. All the recent hysteria over those new strains of the flu didn't phase me; I bypassed getting immunized yet saw a few who were vaccinated become ill.

And I couldn't believe it happened when it did. It was July, *and* it was hotter than July—which meant I couldn't be in an air conditioned room or sleep under a fan.

So, you can imagine what a cranky, fussy, and difficult patient I was.

"Get back in bed," Bobby demanded, for the third time.

"I bet you say that to all the boys."

"Only the ones hacking, like you."

I hacked. "I can't take it anymore. It feels like I've been laying here for weeks."

"It's only been a *day*."

That day turned into a dozen. For the first time since we met, my body didn't have a fever and the room wasn't spinning because Bobby and I were tackling and tagging each other. But he still kept me—this time in different ways.

He kept the hot tea with ginger and honey, orange juice, and chicken noodle soup (which he prepared) coming, serving me something every few hours.

He kept me entertained. We played Monopoly and Blackjack. He did a rather funny lip-synch performance to Lady Gaga's "Born This Way"—then reached back to the original "Born This Way" anthem by Carl Bean, popping and locking as if he were Jeffrey Daniel on *Soul Train*. And he introduced me to the *unreal* reality star antics of Tamar Braxton (whoneedstojustquit.com) and Tami Roman (who needs anger management *and* psychiatric help) during marathons of *Braxton Family Values* and what Bobby said should be called *Basket-*

ball Ex-Wives, Ex-Fiancees, & Ex-Tricks (after watching just one episode, I had to agree).

He even kept me company at night, instead of crashing on the sofa in the very cool living room.

Yes, I loved having a man take care of me. And I loved how *this* man took care of me. But I could tell he *really* loved doing it—and would want to continue doing it.

I was fully healed in time for Marq's annual White Party, held at his three-bedroom co-op in mid-town, the second Saturday in August. I expected (well, more like hoped) that Bobby would attend Fire Island Blackout, sort of a last summer hurrah before heading back to D.C. But he went last year ("I don't like to repeat myself") and already had a me-n-my-boiz bash on the beach at Coney Island.

Naturally, all forty mouths dropped and eighty eyes leered when Bobby and I made our entrance. He was not only the youngest person in the crowd but the youngest person ever to attend the party in the eleven years Marq hosted it. Both of those crowns were previously worn by Marq's spouse, Felix, who is eight years Marq's junior (Marq is the oldest of our trio, but only by a month; he turned 40 on April Fool's Day, while Les and I both joined him on May 1st). Having Bobby on my arm made me feel *grand*; I *relished* the jealousy that registered on a few faces, especially Eldridge DeSouza III, who loved to brag every year about his jaunts to Rio, *the* highlight always being his frolic with some luscious local more than half his age (he's 54 but still tells folks he's fortysomething). And the special attention Bobby paid while I was ill carried over: he got me a drink (with two refills), fixed me a plate, and at one point took a seat next to and kissed me on Marq's midnight blue love seat, a moment captured and christened by Felix (an advertorial photographer for pharmaceutical companies) as "the shot of the night."

But ... while I wanted folks to *see* we were together, I didn't want them to *think* we were together.

Then Cedric walked in.

Cedric is, by all accounts, a Catch: a Harvard Business grad and investment banker whose net worth is in the low eight figures. He owns a townhouse on the Upper West Side and a mansion in Malibu Canyon (where he counts Will & Jada as both neighbors and clients).

Men of his status are usually lacking in the looks department—but he's an exception to that rule. In fact, he used to model in college and the only thing that has changed in the decades since is that the inch-high 'fro has gotten a little gray. He's also maintained that lean, trim bod.

Yet ... have you ever met someone who's got the whole package *and* is your type, but there is no attraction, no spark, no chemistry? That's Cedric and I. For some reason, he just doesn't turn me on. *At all.* For many, he's a show-stopper; for me, he's a *dick*-stopper.

But, on this particular night, he'd make the perfect, unsuspecting foil.

I saw my chance to implement the plan when LeeRoy Burrell, a Dance Theater of Harlem alum, asked if I would mind if he and Bobby boogied to Beyonce. Normally I would: LeeRoy is a *big* flirt. But that would actually work to my advantage. I gave them the green light.

As they set fire to the dance floor, Cedric eased over to me and made his move for the zillionth time.

He grinned. "So, how's my tasty-looking Hershey's Kiss doing?" He asks that every year.

As he continued to say more corny shit, I followed Lee-Roy's lead: when he batted his eyes at Bobby, I did the same with Cedric. When he playfully poked Bobby in the pecs, I did the same with Cedric. When he leaned into and on Bobby (the old trick of pretending not being able to hear so one has to get closer), I did the same with Cedric.

But I took it a step further: I kissed Cedric, very sensuously. At least I *tried* to: There was absolutely no passion in the pucker. *This man is almost fifty years old and he doesn't know how to kiss???*

Bobby noticed—along with one other person.

Marq waltzed over. He smiled at Cedric. "Excuse us." He pinched me on my left arm and pushed me further down the hall towards his bedrooms.

"What the *hell* are you doing?" He was *serious*; as he did with the s and f words, he spelled out h-e-l-l.

"What do you think I'm doing? I'm having a good time."

"With the wrong man."

"You have been trying to get us together for the longest." And he had been, especially during my sex sabbatical.

"So, you decide to get together with him the very first time you bring someone to the party?"

"Right. I brought Bobby *to* the party; he's not *with* me."

"Don't play word games with me. And stop playing with Bobby—*and* Ced."

Les marched up to us. "Why did Bobby just leave—and why aren't you leaving with him?"

"Probably because he doesn't like being disrespected," Marq explained. "*Some*body decided to get all lovey dovey with Ced."

Les looked at me with disgust. "*This* is how you tell him it's over? Foul. Just foul."

"You should talk, swapping them out every three months," I argued.

"Don't get beside yourself: I've *never* swapped them out in front of each other."

"All I was doing was some harmless flirting. LeeRoy was doing it with Bobby."

Marq eyed my nearly empty glass. "Even a *lush* like you knows the difference between harmless flirting and physically assaulting someone with their tongue."

"*You* know better," added Les. "And you need to go after him."

I shrugged. "I am having too much fun."

They didn't say anything else to me the rest of the night. Les left the party without saying good-bye, while Marq disappeared into his bedroom when Cedric and I headed out with the last few remaining guests. Cedric drove me home; I could have invited him up but ... I wasn't in the mood.

Well, I wasn't in the mood for *him*.

For the first time, I was the only one to show up for Tuesday Tea.

I texted both Les and Marq: "Where r u 2?"

Les shot back a two-word retort: "Stunt cunt."

I called him. Of course, he didn't pick up. I was going to leave a message but ... what could I say? That he was wrong?

I called Bobby; I'd only sent him a text the day after the party ("U mad with me?"), which he (not surprisingly) didn't respond to. His voice mail greeting came on: "This is Robert Carpenter, Jr. If this is a business call, please leave a message after the beep; if not, please press 2. Thanks for calling and I'll get back to you as soon as I can. Have a great day."

I pressed 2.

Beep.

"Hi Bobby ... uh ... please call me. Hope to hear from you soon. Bye."

He didn't call back.

Then, one week later, at exactly 1:51 pm, I was having lunch with a co-worker, Gizelle Redding, in the break room for TSA personnel at Terminal 5, JetBlue's hub. That room—that *entire* room—started to shake. That included our chairs and the table our Subway sandwiches and drinks were on.

"Oh my God, what's happening?" Gizelle screamed, jumping into my lap and encasing my head with her arms like the facehugger in the *Alien* series.

I had to maneuver my mouth and nose from under he very ample bosom just to breathe. By the time I caught my breath, the shaking stopped.

Cole O'Hara, another employee, burst into the room. "Did you guys feel that?" He took in the scene. "Whoa. Am I interrupting something?" He knew he couldn't be—we were both gay (as was he).

As Gizelle climbed off of me, I fixed my shirt. "What happened?"

Turned out there was an earthquake in Virginia. The shock was felt all the way up the east coast, even in Canada.

I immediately called Les, who was scheduled to be in D.C. checking out spaces to open his first national Sun Kiss satellite.

"I'm OK," he answered, out of breath.

"You sure? You sound ... "

"Gobsmacked would be the word."

"Where are you?"

"At Union Station. The train pulled in ten minutes ago."

"Is there any damage?"

"Not where I am."

"Is the real estate agent still coming to get you?"

"She texted me a moment ago. She's trying to make her way to me but traffic is at a stand still." He inhaled and exhaled, heavily. "You remembered."

"Of course I did."

Silence.

"See what happens when you treat the boy toy wrong? The earth moves."

We laughed.

Then the following night, newscasters began sounding the alarm about Hurricane Irene heading up the eastern seaboard. The prediction was that she'd hit New York City with a hundred plus mile per hour winds Saturday night. I figured I was safe since I already had an emergency kit (complete with a flashlight, transistor radio, and batteries), and plenty of canned goods and bottled water. But then I turned to a cable broadcast advising residents who lived above the tenth floor in high rise buildings to seek shelter elsewhere: The force and speed of the hurricane could be powerful enough to bust out windows.

I was on the seventeenth floor.

Just seconds after also hearing that dire warning, Marq called. "I'm *still* p-i-s-s-e-d at you, but I don't want you to be swept away by Mz Irene. You *have* to stay with us this weekend."

Since his apartment is on the fourth floor, I appreciated the offer and accepted. But I didn't want to be the third wheel watching he and Felix camped out on that love seat making goo-goo eyes at each other as Irene blew through (the way they neck and nuzzle, you'd think they were love struck teenagers). I hoped to bring a guest with me—and, this time, treat him right.

Of course, that meant really facing the music.

Nekked Boiz Sangin'! moved to the Roy Arias Theater, just steps from the bright lights of Broadway, for a seven weekend, nearly sold-out run. As part of the promotional push, Bobby launched both an *NBS* website and Facebook page (as well as the show's own Twitter account), and went everywhere with a batch of postcards in his back pocket (with Marq's permission, he passed them out at the White Party). And his efforts paid off: the show earned enthusiastic write-ups in *Theatre World* and *The Huffington Post*, and a spotlight on local cable news network NY-1's *On Stage* program (the director, composer, and two of the actors were interviewed; of course, one of those actors was Manuel).

Since Bobby wasn't communicating with me, I figured the invitation to the opening night performance and post-reception was rescinded. How surprised I was when I called the box office and discovered that my name was still on the comp list ...

The show was *much* better the second time around: all of the truly awful songs were dropped and hummable ones were added, while Manuel's role was beefed up with a duet (performed with Corey Corey) on the very catchy "You Show Me Yours, I'll Show You Mine" (it certainly pays when your manager is the producer).

As the cast once again mingled with the audience, I spotted Bobby heading for the exit and followed him into the bathroom. He looked so sharp and sexy in a cream colored shirt, kente patterned bow tie, and brown slacks. His braided hair was still looking crisp.

"Bobby."

He was standing at the stall. He wouldn't even acknowledge me. He zipped up and flushed.

"Can we talk?"

He walked over to the sink. He pushed the soap dispenser down. He lathered his hands, washed them, then held them under the automatic drier.

As he was about to leave, I stepped in front of him. "Please. Hear me out."

He sighed. He crossed his arms. "Talk."

"Uh ... congratulations. I *really* enjoyed the show this time. I like the changes you made."

"You don't want to talk about the show."

"Alright. I ... I wanted to apologize."

"I'm listening."

"I'm sorry for ... acting my shoe size, and not my age."

"That's a good way of putting it."

"The way I ... "

"Showed your ass. And not in a good way."

"In a manner of speaking, yes. It was foul."

"It was."

"I didn't really want to drive you away."

"You didn't? What did you expect to happen? That I would get all bent and clock ol' boy? If you haven't figured it out yet, I have a very low tolerance for bullshit. And I'm a lover, not a fighter."

Don't I know it.

"I got the hint," he continued. "You didn't have to give me your ass to kiss, *twice*. Like Maya Angelou says, 'When people show you who they are, believe them the first time'."

"And ... who did I show you I am?"

"A shady sissy."

I flinched. That hit me right in the gut.

He shrugged. "You asked."

"I did. And ... I *was* being a shady sissy. But that's not who I *am*."

"Then who are you?"

"A man that ... got ... spooked."

"Spooked how?"

"I thought you wanted something more."

"More than what?"

"More than ... what we had."

"Did I ever say, 'This is my side of the bed?' Did I ask for a key? Did I leave my drawers in your clothes hamper for you to wash?"

"No."

"So why would you think that?"

I went straight to the initial trigger. "What about your bringing up Mitchell and Raheim's relationship?"

"Can't a brutha make conversation?"

"You said you wanted what they have."

"Right. I said I wanted what they have; I didn't say I wanted it with *you*."

Gut punch #2. I nodded.

He flicked his chin with his left thumb, which meant he was thinking. "Were you also spooked by my nursing you back to health?"

"I ... suppose."

"*Damn*. What was I supposed to do, leave you high and dry to fend for yourself? Even a jump-off deserves to be treated with respect."

"When you say jump-off, you mean ... "

"I guess that would be fuck buddy in your language. Although, in your case, I guess it'd also be a jump-*on* and a jump-*in*."

"Well, no matter what we call it, I still want to be that."

"Do you?"

"Yes."

"Well, you got a fucked up way of showing it. Why?"

"Because ... I like you. And I like being with you. And ... I miss you."

"You ... miss me?"

I nodded yes.

He searched my eyes; *could he tell I was being sincere?* "What about the distance?"

"DC is just a few hours away."

His left eyebrow rose; it was a sign his interest had been piqued. "You're gonna visit me?"

"If that's what I gotta do."

"What about your intimacy issues?"

Intimacy issues. Marq would call it my *commitment-phobia.* But the fact that I've gone past the two-year cut-off with TSA and I've run back to a lover for the very first time might mean the spell has been broken. *Maybe.* "They are *my* intimacy issues. I won't project them on to you."

"And, if you got a question, you won't ass-u-me?"

"I won't."

He just stared.

"So ... will you give me another chance?"

Bobby glanced down. He grabbed my right pinky with his left. "I suppose I can crush on you some more."

We kissed. *Lawdy, could he give Cedric some lessons ...*

He gently pushed me against the door with his own body. "But, remember: Just 'cause I'm crazy for you doesn't mean I'm gonna let you drive me crazy."

"I'm crazy for you, too."

"No, you're just *crazy.*" There was that twinkle in his eyes and that little boy giggle.

"So, what are you doing after the after-party?"

He grabbed my ass. "*You.* You got some makin' up to do."

I grabbed his. "Yes, I do."

BOOTY, BY JAKE

This is the story of the dick that *almost* got away ...

I met him—well, I didn't *meet* him because we never formally introduced ourselves, but we'll just say I did—the evening I moved into my new apartment in the East Point section of Atlanta. Like many Black gay men, I ventured to the ATL for the opportunities—business *and* pleasure. After being born, raised, and spending my twenties living paycheck to paycheck in the Big Apple, I took a management position with Ace Deuce, a wholesale electronics merchandiser. The salary was only $15,000 a year more, but I'd enjoy a slower, quieter way of life and could save enough green for a down payment on my first home. Which made the one-bedroom apartment I was moving into so perfect: it was two miles from the job, a three minute walk from the MARTA station (the gas-guzzling Wrangler would stay home during the week), and the rent was only $475 a month—$400 less than what I was shelling out (*with* a roommate) in Park Slope, Brooklyn. Of course, it was smaller (not even 600 square feet) and in a working class area (not ghetto but struggling to reach middle class), but it was clean, convenient, and cheap.

A native named Nestle (yes, as in Crunch) wanted to officially welcome me to the city and help me "christen" my new pad (he had a taste when I was in town a month before interviewing for the position; he liked). *I don't mind*, I told him, *so long as you bring your own damn condoms* (he claimed he "forgot" them the last time when I made it clear I didn't have any, so the groove was disturbed while he went to purchase some; but he made up for it when he returned, nailin' me against the hotel room sink). I popped into the local Kroger for a few items (Poland Spring for me, Miller Lite for him, whipped cream and strawberries for us both to nibble on and off of each other) and was on my way into the building when I noticed him. He wore a forest green polyester short sleeve button down shirt and slacks; I (correctly) assumed he was the super.

He wasn't my type. Too ... ordinary. Looking. Might be the kind of gent you'd glance at but not the kind you'd *peep*. I'm not conceited but I know I look hellafied good. The boiz (*and* girlz) don't just look my way; they *leer*. Thanks to a four-day-a-week gym regiment, I have a bumpin' frame to go with the flawless face and marquee smile.

I'm on the A-List; sometimes I *am* the A-List. He's straddling B and C. Not ugly, not unattractive. Just ... average.

He was too short. I'm six feet; he's around 5' 9". You gotta be, at minimum, eye level to mash my monster.

He was too dark. Not that there's anything wrong with chocolate. I'm honey mustard and prefer the milk-in-my-coffee variety.

I'm a Will Smith; he's a Don Cheadle. Very different men in very different leagues (it didn't register that Don appeared on an episode of *The Fresh Prince of Bel-Air* and the chemistry between he and Will was undeniable; uh-huh, the writing was on the wall).

He was seated against the hood of a tore up tan station wagon (a *Pimp My Ride* candidate if there ever was one), which went with those tore up, unfastened Timbs. A toothpick sat between his purplish lips.

I smiled. "Evening."

He nodded. He half-smiled. "Evenin'," he mumbled.

But when I passed him, he perked up and that Georgia twang came out. "*Day-um.* Bet there ain't nuthin' in that sack tastier than that azz."

I stopped, but shouldn't have. I turned, but shouldn't have. There he was, wearing that smug-ass grin. He pegged me. He had me. And he knew it.

Every other day, he reminded me.

"Ya hurtin' me, son."

"You got me feenin', yo."

"You fillin' in them jeans nice, bruh."

"Now, wha'cha go and wear *that* for?"

"I got what you need."

Yeah. Right.

We're the only people on the elevator; he has to stand directly behind me.

"What are you doing?"

"What you think?"

"Will you please back up?"

"We on the same page, yo. I was gonna ask *you* to do the same thang." There's that smug-ass grin.

I'm checking my mail box (which I have to crunch down to do) and he's either standing a few feet away in the lobby area or outside peeking through the glass, enjoying the view. With that smug-ass grin.

I'm doing my laundry. He calls himself checking the water pressure or cleaning the lint from the dryers or sweeping up or emptying the trash. All the while wearing that smug-ass grin.

Once my tub backed up and Drain-o wasn't cutting it. He came in with his ... snake.

"So, *Ray*: any other pipe you need me to *lay*?" he inquired after the job was done.

As he stood there, wearing that smug-ass grin, I shut the door.

And mornings after I entertained, he was yackin' the same refrain ...

"That dude can't manage you."

"Excuse me?" I finally responded after ignoring him a half-dozen times before.

"That dude can't manage you."

"What does that mean?"

"Like you don't know."

"Why are you up in my business?"

"You put me up in it."

"Hunh?"

"You deaf or what, yo? How come I gotta repeat shit? Always got some dude leavin' when I'm 'round."

"Maybe that's because you're always lurking about, spying on me."

"Say what?"

"Now *you're* deaf?"

"Don't trip."

"You're the one trippin'. Like I care if you're around?"

"Course you do."

"Mother-fucker, please."

"I *am* a mother-fucker. I'm a *father*-fucker, too. You ain't neither one," he snickered.

No. He. Didn't. "Don't *fuckin'* worry about what I am!"

"I ain't gotta worry. I'm clear on it."

"And how the hell would *you* know what he can manage? He manages *this* very well." The "he" in this case was a semi-regular (every other week) named Lavon, another east coast transplant (Newark) who was the right height, the right weight, the right shade, *and* the right size.

He scoffed. "Very well? Why you settlin' for that?"

I frowned. There was that smug-ass grin, again.

Now, it's often said that homos are 10% of the population; in Atlanta, the reverse is true. I feel for the straight sisters; their pickins are *very* slim, for even a good percentage of those men who *are* straight (i.e., not "straight acting" or DL) will swing it your way depending on their mood, the weather, the time of day or night, whether they got paid and, naturally, whether they got laid by their lady. Which is why ATL is the Land of Horny Plenty: It doesn't have the kind of ethnic and cultural diversity of New York (the true rainbow capitol of the world) but there are a bountiful supply of other Black men to be horny plenty with. Unfortunately, ATL is also dubbed the Land of a Million Bottoms, and boiz who can really put it down are premium (so much so that some auction the dick off on sites like adam4adam). And, there are times when even an A-Lister will find himself on hold or on the shelf, waiting to be taken off (and *taken*).

Like me. On the night in question, I was burnin' to be blazed (I usually get tagged once a week but had gone without for twenty consecutive days), none of the regulars (including the very reliable Lavon) could be found, and everyone I hit up on-line had other plans (i.e., somebooty else to bang). It was too late to venture to Lenox Mall (Saturday is not the only day of the week the boiz turn it into an unofficial Black gay club) and falling up in any of the usual meating spots like Bulldogs or 708 was *out* of the question (I only frequent them to drink and/or dance—and that's it). So, after three hours, I resigned myself to spending the rest of the evening sucking on half a box of Edy's whole fruit mixed bars (the only thing that can cool me down when I'm hot and can't get off). I was about to unwrap the third (and final) bar when I peered out my bedroom window and caught him standing in front of his raggedy ass car, his left foot up on the fender.

Is that ... ? No. Is that ... ? It is!

His very fat dick head was peeking out of his shorts (actually, they were swimming trunks). Even in the dark from the third floor, it was very visible and very big. Before standing upright, he shifted the dick, so that it fell sideways and out further.

And my ass went: *womp, womp, womp.*

Talk about traveling faster than the speed of light: I zoomed past the elevator, jetted down the stairs, and was outside in less than a minute. I nodded at him; he nodded back. I jogged over to my car, which was parked two spaces down from his. I pretended to look inside the glove compartment for something. After thirty seconds, I exited the car and was about to reenter the building when ...

"Why you playin', son? We know what's up."

This time I was happy I stopped—and turned. And, for the first time, happy to see that smug-ass grin.

I don't recall *how* we got upstairs but the next thing I remember is him posed in the middle of my living area, arms crossed against his chest, the pelvis thrust forward, the dick just pulsating and ready to be revealed. I was salivating, *literally* salivating with anticipation (the liquid dripped over my bottom lip and hit the hardwood floor with a splash). I had the honor of unsheathing his sword. I fell on my right knee and pulled down the shorts.

O. Muh. Gohd.

It was prettier in person. And just so ... *perfect.* Long. Thick. And *crooked!* It bends slightly to the left in the center—*just* like I love 'em. And that head ... *oh that head!* Just a sittin' on top like a crown. Like the dick, the balls were hairless, bumpless, and *smooth* as an orange skin. In fact, the whole area had the aroma of an orange.

What do you know ... my favorite fruit.

I let my nose travel along the head, the shaft, the pubic area, and the balls; it grew some more and he snarled. Then I let my tongue retrace the route; it grew even more and he snarled a little louder. I repeated steps 1 and 2 (I can't say how many times), fluttered with the foreskin (sucking from the inside out, eliciting grunts and huffs), and gnawed on that sack (hello, no mouth full of Brillo!) until every area was spit-shine polished and he was so ready to be pumped. I gobbled him up.

The dick is on a downward slope, which meant if I tilted my head up and slightly to the side at *just* the right angle, he could fuck my face so wondrously. You know I could and you know he did. No pressure, no force. My tongue teased and lips popped the head, causing him to shudder every time.

Now *this* is what you call a stimulus package.

I could've gorged on it all night—the aroma, the sweat, the pre-cum made it all so fuckin' scrumdickliscious—but he had other ideas (thank God).

He had already dropped the trunks and flung off his wife beater; he was ripped from shoulder blade to calf (naturally, the Timbs would remain on). I only had the chance to pull my shorts under my ass and balls (I was busy doing other important things, after all) when ...

"Lay back, yo. I wanna snack on that azz."

You got it.

I'm a member of the Lil' Kim fan club: No licky licky, no sticky sticky. Problem is, half these boiz don't do it, and too many of those that do don't really know *how* to. It's an ass, you fool, not a lollipop or popsicle. Don't just lick it; lap up in it. Let me feel it. Let me *hear* it. Put your face, your neck, your shoulders, your *whole* body into it.

Jake did just that. As soon as my back contacted the floor and the legs went up, and before I could pull my shorts up and fling them (along with my sandals) over my head, he had begun his expedition, first poking his nose in where it did belong and heaving a warm breeze up through the tunnel that made my insides *quiver*, inhaling me as the lips puckered up, and the tongue darted in and out, in and around, in and out, in and around. He pushed his face further and further and *further* in, eating me out like it was his Last Supper, as my yelps of *"Oh," "Ooh,"* and *"Oomph"* became lighter and higher.

He wasn't snackin' it; he was *mackin'* it.

I was about to lose my mind (and my seed) when, without breaking his lickety concentration, his palms made contact with my cheeks and he gently pushed me forward. I knew what *that* meant, and I knew what to do: cuff my arms under the back of my knees and curl in. When I glanced up, he was already *ready*: the condom was on.

His dick found its own way and nudged right on in—and *down*.

Lawd a mercy.

The great things about the floor: (1) it doesn't move, (2) you can't fall off, and (3) whoever is fuckin' can *really* tear it up. And Jake knew the deal: his technique was outstanding, his frequency consistent, his precision steady, and his delivery always *on*, allowing that hook to travel deeper, and deeper, and *deeper* inside.

Now, too many of these boiz think that because they top means they are *on* top. *This my azz, I'm runnin' thangz, I'm Top Dawg, I'm Da Man.* Uh-huh.

So. They. Think.

Just because I give it up like it's pussy don't mean I *am* a pussy. Which is why they get all up in it and get all twisted when *I* twist it ...

"What the fuck, yo!"

"Damn, let up on it nigga!"

"Whoa, bitch! Lemme breathe, *lemme breathe!"* (Uh-huh. Who's the *bitch* now?)

But Jake.

Oh Jake.

Oh Jake!

Oh Jake!

No amount of twistin' turned him; all it did was turn *me*. That swirl on the downstroke, that bump on the up; that hump on the way back down, the grind on the way back up ... he was *murderin'* it. And I was *lovin'* it—and I had to let him know it.

"Oh Jake, don't make me scream."

"Oh Jake, don't make me scream!"

"Oh, Jake, don't make me scream!"

Now, how silly is *that* shit? He had me *screaming*—and I was demanding that he *not* make me scream. He just wasn't hittin' *the* spot—he found that immediately—he was hittin' spots I never knew existed. And hittin' 'em, and hittin' 'em, and hittin' 'em *right* ...

And *that* was just the warm-up. He was on stroke #106 (yeah, I counted) when he gripped and lifted me around the waist, marched into the bedroom, plopped me down on the left corner of the bed, and continued jackhammerin' that azz.

Some of these boiz get up in it and want to set up house. No, I don't mind them coming in and rearranging the furniture, doing some detail work, even loosening up a few screws. Go on, make yourself comfortable and make *me* comfortable.

But Jake? He was trying to do a gut rehab—knocking down the walls, repaving the floors, just remodeling the whole damn thang.

Blow. Ing. It. Up.

So I continued to *scream*. And, while dirty talk bores me (don't you hate it when the other person is giving you a play by play of what's going down—as if *you're* not right there experiencing it with them?), I found myself shouting things I never *thought* of before (*"Yeah*, beat that pussy *up!"* "Lay it out, mother-fucker," and my fave, *"Break it down, Jake, break it on down!"*). But he was paying me *dust*. He didn't crack a smile.

Or a smirk. Not even his trademark grin. In fact, he didn't look in my direction. He was *serious* about and only focused on the azz. He was on the job, managing it like he knew he could, like only *he* could.

I've had ... well, my share of dicks in this life. Some good, some bad; some indifferent, some just plain sad. Some that set me on fire; too many that were t-*ired*. A select few, excellent. A couple, magnifique.

But Jake? Not ridiculous. Not sick. Ri*dick*ulously sick. *I'm a believer, Jake. I'm a believer.*

I was so wrapped up that I lost count. The third go 'round I got to stroke (what do you know?) #69 and gave up—and totally gave *it* up.

And that's when he let out a growl that scared me, pulled out, pulled off the condom, and *blew the fuck up*, releasing a mound of gooey jizz on my chest for over three minutes (I checked the clock).

Then he knew just what to do to help me blow: he finished mushin' my monster. It was his dessert—and I provided a very special brand of whipped cream.

But then I came down—and came back to reality. Besides that intense pulse in the pusswah, I was feeling ... what was it ... regret? *Damn* ... how come the head above the neck couldn't be as fly as the one below the waist? What I had always dismissed as a myth had revealed itself to be true: you *can* get hot sex from the not-so-hot.

I was also angry (not with him but at him) because he made me break two of my rules: don't do the help and don't do the neighbors (he lived, rent free, in the building next door). I dreaded what was on the horizon: expecting to see me whenever he wanted, confronting any man who leaves my place, thinking that because he had a piece he owns the pie.

I looked over to the bookshelf; that's where I left the other fruit bar. It was now grape liquid. "Now what?"

"I'm in yo' bed. I do what you want."

Say what? I turned my head to the left. "What did you say?"

"You back to not hearin' again? Musta knocked yo' ear drums out." He chuckled. "I'm in yo' bed, I do what you want."

Mmm ... a man had never been in my bed and, after doin' the do, said something so ... profound. So ... selfless. So ... romantic? It was the greeting card, the candy, *and* the flowers. *Hmm* ... he ain't fine but he could be a fine investment.

At that moment, he jumped onto the A-List.

He leaned in and on me, pressing hard, the dick settling between my cheeks; must be his idea of a hug. Felt ... nice.

I moaned. "Well ... I'd love it if you'd wear my ass out again."

His dick heard me—it began poking me.

Yup, he was wearing that smug-ass grin. I was, too.

BALLS & CHAIN

What you do that to me for?

Because.

Because, why?

Because, I want you to love me.

Man, I already love you.

You do?

Of course I do. You my li'l cuz, my li'l man. You know I love you, right?

I ... I guess so.

You guess? You don't have to guess about a thing like that, Dre. Ya hear me?

I do.

Good. And, you don't do things to people so they love you—especially somethin' like *that*. Uh ... you ever do that to somebody else so they would love you?

Um ... yes.

Who?

Uh ...

You can tell me. I won't tell nobody.

Uncle Petie.

What? He asked you to do that so he would love you?

Yes. You mad at me.

No, Dre, I ain't mad at you.

Yes you are. Aunt Jessie said that your forehead wrinkles when you get mad.

I ain't mad at you; I'm mad at Uncle Petie. *Damn.* He been touchin' you?

Touching me?

Yeah. You know ...

You mean, touching my pee-wee?

Yeah.

No.

He never touched you there?

No. Mama always told me not to let anybody touch me there.

Did he suck your pee-wee?

No.

Did he try to suck it?

No.

Ah. He slick. What did he ask you to do?

Um ...

You can tell me. You can tell me anything.

Uh, he asked me to play with his balls and chain.

That mutha-fucka. He still up to his old tricks.

Whatcha mean?

Nothin'. Dre, you don't have to do that to him again. And you don't have to do it to me, neither.

But why? Didn't it make you feel good?

Uh ... huh?

It made you feel good.

What, what makes you think that?

Because, you were huffing and puffing, like Uncle Petie. And you were making moaning noises, like Uncle Petie. And pushing my head down on it harder and harder, like Uncle Petie. And the milk squirted out of your big-wee, like Uncle Petie.

Man, I ... I did all that because ... I thought I was drea-min'.

You was asleep?

Not all the way, but it felt like I was. You know how sometimes you be dreamin' and it feels so real, like you can actually feel what's goin' on?

Uh-huh.

That's how it was for me. But I ain't realize until, like you said, my milk was gonna squirt that it was real. When you grow up you'll see that a big-wee has a mind of its own.

Oh. So, it didn't make you feel good?

Man. Let's put it this way: you made my *big-wee* feel good. But just because you made it feel good don't mean that what you did was good.

Whatcha mean?

What I mean is, you shouldn't be doin' that to me or Uncle Petie or anybody else. You done it to anybody else?

No.

Nobody?

No.

You sure? You can tell me.

I'm sure. Just you and Uncle Petie.

Good. Don't ever do it again.

Why?

Because it ain't right.

Why?

Because, a boy ain't supposed to do that.

Why?

Because, a boy shouldn't be suckin' on a grown man's dick, that's why.

You not a grown man.

Or a *young* man's dick. Boys, young men, grown men get their pee-wees and big-wees sucked by females.

But Uncle Petie says that boys do it best.

Don't be listenin' to what he say. He just a pervert.

A per-vert?

Yeah. That's what you call somebody like him, a grown man who messes around with kids.

Messes around?

Yeah. Gets them to do dirty things that a kid shouldn't be doin', like suckin' on big-wees.

So ... it's dirty to suck on big-wees?

For a boy, yeah.

But Uncle Petie—

Just forget everything he ever told you. He would tell you anything to get you to suck him off. He ain't nothin' but a punk, anyway.

A punk?

Yeah.

What's a punk?

That's a man or a boy that likes other men or boys.

Uh ... that's a bad thing?

Yeah.

But ...

But what?

I ... I like boys.

Huh? What makes you think that? You only 8.

Because, I do.

You *think* you like a lot of things and then you don't. Like, you wanted to be a fireman last month, remember?

Yes.

And now what you wanna be?

A airline pilot.

See. You just learning about things, discoverin' what's in the world. So what you like is always gonna be changin'.

Um ... but I really do like boys.

Maybe you do today, but you won't tomorrow.

And I really like to suck on big-wees.

And you only like doin' that 'cause Uncle Petie made you.

No he didn't.

He did, Dre. He ain't hold a gun to your head and said 'Do it or else', but he still made you do it.

Whatcha mean?

You a kid, and—

I'm a *big* kid.

Right. You a *big* kid, but you still a kid. And he a adult. And adults like him know that kids are taught to obey their elders. So he knew if he asked you to do it in the right way, you would. Did he grab you by the shoulders and force you to do it?

No. He was really nice. He even let me play with his big-wee. He said it could be my new toy.

See what I mean. He wanted you to see it as somethin' to play with, so you would like to do it. And that's why you say you like it. If he had forced you and was mean or angry about it or said he'd spank you if you didn't, you probably wouldn't say you like it.

Um ... but I liked to suck on your big-wee the most.

You ... did?

Uh-huh.

Uh ... what made you wanna suck it?

I saw it when I was taking a bath. You came into the bathroom to take a tinkle. Yours is bigger than Uncle Petie's. And it points straight, like a arrow. Uncle Petie, his is crooked. And yours taste better, too.

It *taste* better? *Man* ...

You ever suck on a big-wee?

No.

If you did, you would like it, too.

I don't think so.

My favorite part is when the milk shoots out. That's fun. It's sticky and warm. Yours is really gooey. Uncle Petie's, his milk isn't.

Dre, it ain't supposed to be fun and you ain't supposed to like it.

Why not?

Because, like I said, it ain't right. Boys ain't supposed to do that to other boys. You don't want people to say you a bad boy, do you?

No.

Well, if they find out you do that or like that ... they gonna think you are. That's why Uncle Petie told you not to tell nobody.

How you know he said that?

Because, he don't want nobody to know that he got you suckin' on his big-wee. And it ain't right to be sneakin' into people's beds, doin' stuff like that.

Oh. So ... I'm a bad boy?

No, you not a bad boy. But what you been doin' to him and what you did to me is bad. That's why you can't do it no more. To nobody. You understand?

I ... I think so.

Now, don't tell anybody about what you did tonight or what you did with Uncle Petie. I'll keep everything secret too. 'Cause if anybody finds out, Uncle Petie will be in trouble. He gonna go to jail.

Jail?

Yeah. It's against the law for him to be messin' with a kid. And you will be in trouble, too.

You mean, I'm gonna go to jail?

Nah, nah, Dre. You'll be in a different kind of trouble.

A different kind?

Yeah. People will treat you bad. And they'll call you bad names.

Like ... punk?

Yeah. And some of them may even wanna hurt you.

Hurt me?

Yeah. Hit you, punch you, beat you up.

But why?

Because, they hate boys who mess around with men.

Oh.

And you don't want nobody to hate you, do you?

No.

Well then. Don't say nothin'.

OK. I won't tell.

Good.

But what if Uncle Petie wants me to suck his big-wee again?

Don't you worry about that. He ain't gonna ask you again. I'm gonna make sure of that.

A KISS IS JUST A KISS

We were sweaty and sticky, lying on our backs, shoulder blades and forearms rubbing, his left leg looped around my right, my right thumb flicking his left nipple, the funky yet intoxicating aroma of another fresh fuck settling in the air like incense.

The script called for him to catch a very brief nap, no more than a half hour. So, like I always did, I stared at the ceiling fan, which was sending down a comfortable stream of air that was beginning to cut through the heat produced just minutes before, and basked in the afterglow.

But then, instead of his light snore, I heard and felt belabored breathing, traveling from my neck to my cheek. I turned quickly to my right. We were nose to nose.

He kissed me. Well, it really wasn't a kiss: he pressed his lips into mine and withdrew.

He seemed surprised at what he had done; he looked away, somewhat embarrassed. "Ah. Sorry."

"For what?"

"For that."

"Why are you sorry?"

"'Cause. That's goin' against the grain."

"You mean *your* grain," I corrected him.

"Yeah."

We both studied the ceiling fan.

"Why did you do it?" I asked.

"Just felt like it."

"*Why* did you feel like it?"

He shrugged. "Seemed like ... the thing to do."

Not *the right thing*, just *the thing*.

We laid there, neither one of us sure what to say next.

He finally broke that uncomfortable silence. "Uh ... I'ma hop in the shower."

He never made that announcement before. Was he waiting for permission? Apparently so: He was still in bed.

I turned. "OK."

He hustled into the bathroom. As he showered, I dialed up Thomas, my best friend.

"*Ooh ...*" Thomas cooed.

"Ooh what?"

"You got him."

"No, his wife got him."

"Ha, if she *really* had him, he wouldn't be coming to your place every Wednesday after work. First he asks you what your favorite color is ... "

That would be purple.

"Then he wants to know who your favorite actor is—and he brings over one of his movies the following week, to watch with you."

And it was the one movie starring Tommy Lee Jones that I hadn't seen: *Man of the House*.

"Then he got his ass on his shoulders over your sleeping with somebody else ... "

Don't be givin' up my stuff to nobody.

Your ... stuff.

Yeah, my stuff.

My stuff, as you call it, don't belong to you.

Yes it do.

It's your stuff when you in it; when you not, it ain't.

I'm gonna know.

Know what?

If somebody else been up in that azz.

And when they are?
When they are?
Yes, when. What you gonna do?
I ain't gonna have it.
Ha, you won't—he will.
You comical.
No, I'm correct.

" ... now, this. Next thing you know you'll be doing his laundry."

"*Hell* no. This ain't that kind of party, and he knows it."

"What a man *knows* and what a man *feels* are almost always two totally different things. If he doesn't come back next Wednesday, you'll know he can't handle this. But if he *does*, can *you* handle it?"

Oz isn't the biggest I've had. He isn't the longest I've had. And he isn't even the cutest I've had (yes, some dicks are so pretty that they should be declared works of art). But he puts it on down. Not just down, but *on down*. Every Wednesday, we mess around—and then he leaves my bathroom a mess. The first couple of times I contemplated telling him not to return, but you think I'm gonna let a soapy wash cloth left in the sink, a crumpled towel on the floor, or a toilet seat sprinkled with piss get in the way of the very best sex I've ever had? A dick is not hard to find, but a *good* dick is.

Let the church say ... *amen.*

Besides, I had to go through too much and wade through too many triflin' ass Negroes to get to him.

There were those who knew nothing about time: they'd show up an hour or two late and catch a *serious* attimatude when I wouldn't let them in.

There were those that would strike the *I'm da man* pose: laying back with their palms behind their heads to get their *other* heads serviced, as if they were at a filling station. I'd do all the work and they'd act all impressed with themselves as if *they* just performed some wondrous feat.

There were the pretty boys: so handsome on the outside and so hollow on the inside. If he was a true gym bunny, forget it: chances are that his dick had shrunk to the size of a walnut because of all the protein shakes, supplements, stimulants, and steroids ingested. All meat and no potato.

There were those who, after taking the dick out and making terrific use of it, would have their *hands* out. "Yo, can you spot me twenty bills?" *Hell, no*; what the fuck do I look like, Bank of America?

And then there was Tyrell: 24, no job, no high school diploma or G.E.D., straight out of the Pen (a nine month sentence for disorderly conduct, indecent exposure—i.e., urinating in public—and possession of marijuana, for the second time). Naturally, he needed a place to crash for a couple of weeks while he figured out his next move. Said he was straight but didn't mind the attention he received from other men—so, I wasn't at all shocked when he "accidentially" found himself in my bed that second night. And it didn't matter what he called himself 'cause he had no problem gettin' it on and gettin' me off (he wouldn't suck the dick but slopped on the head; guess he figured that, if he didn't let his lips travel down the shaft, he could still call himself straight).

One night he had me going so damn good—I was bouncing on that dick with a *purpose*, you hear me?—that I actually came for the very first time without myself or someone else jerking me. Just watching my dick act and react on its own ... it almost made me come undone.

But of course, *he* was the one that came undone.

As I continued cuming on his chest, he pushed me back and off of him. *"Yo wha' da fuck, nigga! Nah nah, I ain't say you could do dat shit! You just came out da box wit' dat shit!"*

I'd never been ... *scolded* for spilling my seed. A few had frowned upon it (for some of these he-man types, *their* climax is the only important ending to the encounter) but if I also managed to reach that plateau, they didn't begrudge me the pleasure. I never thought I'd be with a man and he'd actually exclaim that he didn't give me permission to satisfy myself. The truth was that *he* had satisfied me in a way no man had ever done before—and that was probably what scared him the most. He could no longer call himself straight if the man he was with reached an orgasm like a woman.

Needless to say, his two week-stay ended five days early.

Oz broke that losers streak. We met on an unseasonably cool Friday in July. I spotted his beefy brown bod nearly half a city block away (34th Street, across the street from Macy's). I was walking east, he west. As he got closer, that Aretha Franklin lyric popped in my head: "Knew you'd be a vision in white, how'd you get your pants so tight?" That thick sausage slinking down his right thigh gave me a tingle in the tookie.

All meat and *lots* of potato.

After eyeing me through his sunglasses, he didn't do the usual gentleman cruise: passing by and walking a few paces before turning to see if I was also checking him out. As soon as we were side by side, he stopped, dropped the glasses down a notch, and took in the view from the back.

"Damn," he declared, loud enough for me and others around to hear.

Many men have had the same reaction to my ass—the kind they'd want to thank my Mama for blessing me with—but no one had ever been as bold in expressing their appreciation for it in public. *A man who knows what he likes and lets you know it.* He had my attention.

He went in for the kill. "'sup, man?"

"'sup?"

"What you gettin' into?"

"Got no plans."

"You got some now."

We were at my place in a half hour. We didn't exchange first names until *after* we took care of the biz—and did Oz know how to take care of the biz! I'd been fucking for twenty years (ever since, at the age of 15, I was seduced by my 24-year-old cousin, Kurt, in a poppy field during a summer visit to Richmond), and most (including Kurt) didn't know how to handle it. No, not handle it—*treat* it. But Oz knew how.

Oz is my independent contractor—and I am his freelance gig. He's never missed a Wednesday. Never. Not even when there's been torrential rains or hundred-plus degree temps. Not even when that two feet of snow fell the week of Christmas 2010 (it took him two hours to *get here*—and, yeah, it was *so* worth it). He's even scheduled his out-of-town trips—visiting the in-laws in Chicago, attending his brother's graduation from law school in Cali, even hopping on the very last flight out of JFK to New Orleans so he could be a pallbearer at his grandfather's funeral the next morning—around our rendezvous.

So the scenes that arose outside of our sexcapades were easy to ignore or explain away. The favorite color came up because he noticed I wore a lot of purple; he was only inquiring about the obvious and mentioned it in passing.

As for the movie: I was feeling a little under the weather and told him I'd make it up to him the following week, but he still insisted on coming over to keep me company. And, since we couldn't partake in our usual activity, he provided us with alternative entertainment. And it wasn't as if he was trying to get all romantic while watching it (he sat in the easy chair and I was on the sofa, several feet apart). To further prove that that was just a fluke: it happened six months ago and he's never mentioned it or suggested we do it again.

And the possessive stance was ... well, Oz just being a man. That's how many of them get when they know they got a good thing goin' and want to keep it to and for themselves. Act like they *discovered* you, you're *their* territory, and no one else can visit the lay of their land. After Oz's outburst, I was still a little miffed (that whole "You mine" syndrome is so high school) but also felt ... flattered. *I ain't gonna have it.* That's right, stake your claim, you knuckle-draggin' neanderthal.

But the kiss was a whole 'nother show, Oprah.

After scrubbing up, Oz didn't say another word about the kiss and left. And, he didn't come back the following Wednesday.

He called me on Tuesday.

"Yo," he shouted.

At first I didn't recognize his voice; I never hear it until Wednesday. "Oz?"

"Who else?"

"Uh, what—"

"I gotta see you."

"Tomorrow."

"Nah, nah, tonite."

"Tonight?"

"Yeah."

"Why?"

"'Cause."

"'Cause why?"

"'Cause, like I said, I just gotta."

I told him to drop by at seven. He was waiting for me, sitting on the stoop of my building (a four floor walk-up in Hell's Kitchen).

"You're a half hour early," I announced.

He held up a yellow plastic bag. "Got us some dinner."

Uh-oh. I recognized the bag and the smell: triple delight from Oodle Noodle, my favorite Chinese restaurant. I told him that, in passing, months ago. It's my Tuesday night meal; I'd usually finish the leftovers on Wednesday after he leaves.

He set out the white containers, plates, and plastic utensils. *Instead of him eating me, we're going to actually eat?*

"This is good," he chomped. "I see why you love it so much."

They were the only words spoken during the meal.

"Thanks," I expressed, as he cleared the table.

"You welcome." He stood by the sink, twiddling his thumbs. "Uh, can we talk?"

I nodded yes.

"Let's sit on the sofa," he instructed.

I complied.

He stroked his very thin goatee. "I ... I wanna say somethin'."

He had *that* look. *Uh-oh, here it comes ...*

"Iloveyou," he rushed out.

"Noyoudon't," I rushed right back.

He was thrown by my response. "How you gonna say that?"

"'Cause you don't. And you *can't.*"

"Why not?"

"You don't even know me."

"I know enough."

"You could never know enough. And you certainly don't know much."

"I *do* love you," he protested.

"You *might* love what I do."

"Nah nah, it's bigger than that, man."

I laughed. I looked down at his crotch. "Yeah, it usually is."

"Come on, man. I'm serious."

"So am I. You love your wife."

"I love her, too."

"You love *her*. You only want *me*."

"I wanna be with you."

"Well, you can't be."

"You don't love me?"

"Of course not."

"That's not what you said a coupla weeks ago."

Is he crazy? "Pardon me?"

"You said you did."

"When?"

"In bed."

"*You* are hearin' things. I didn't say I love *you*; I said I love your *dick*."

"Same thing."

"Don't be ridiculous. Like, tellin' your wife 'I love you' and 'I love your pussy' is the same thing? Get the fuck outa here." I sighed. "This ain't gonna work anymore."

"What?"

"You heard me. You got to go, and don't come back."

"Why?"

"Either you are really catching feelings or you've deluded yourself. Either way, there's no room in this arrangement for either."

"Why can't we just flip the script?"

"Because it's not the script I signed up for." I was becoming heated. "You come here to fuck and only fuck. Now you done fucked it up for the both of us."

"We still got a good thing goin'—"

"We *had* a good thing goin'. Even if we continued on, things would never be the same. You'd probably be hoping for something more and I'd resent you for it. And you'd end up resenting me for not reciprocating."

"How you know?"

"Because I have been in that position, hoping for something more and not getting it. I'm not goin' down this road—"

"Ozwald? Ozwald?" The voice came from outside.

We both froze.

"I know you're up there! You and your *friend*, Christopher, would want to let me up!"

Oh. Shit.

This just could *not* be happening. Somehow, someway, somewhere, Oz slipped up. How else could she find out he was fooling around and *who* he was doing it with? The only thing he'd revealed about his wife was that she was the only person who called him by his first name; even his own parents opted for Oz.

"Ozwald? Don't make me stand down here calling for you all night, 'cause you *know* I will!"

Oz searched my face for an answer as to what he should do. I didn't want her down there disturbing the peace but I also didn't want her up in my apartment. Yet ... her coming was proof that she was going to fight for her man. And I had some news for her: she didn't have to do any fighting, she could have him. Best she hear it from me and take her husband out of my bed and out of my life forever. Yeah, my Wednesdays would never be—and my ass would never *feel*—the same, but I'll have to get over it.

"Let her upstairs."

As Oz ventured downstairs, I went into the kitchen, opened the tool drawer and pulled out both my pepper spray and brass knuckles. If she planned on gettin' ridiculous up in my house, she'd be in for a surprise.

But as it turned out, *I* was the one that was in for a surprise.

They came into the apartment going at it, although he was more upset than she was.

"How you find me?" he barked.

"Like it matters?"

"You been followin' me?"

"Ne-gro, please. Like I ain't got better things to do with my time. I left tracking your cheatin' ass to the expert: our son."

A son? Oz never mentioned he had children.

"O.J.? What he gotta do with this?"

"He got eyes, and knows how to use Google."

"You told him?"

"*He* told *me*, fool. But then, he didn't have to: not only do I have eyes, I have a very strong sense of *smell*."

Guess those showers couldn't get rid of all our funk ...

Her eyes fell on me. "So ... you're Christopher."

"I am."

She looked me over, approvingly. She glanced at her husband. "At least he ain't no sissy. I'd want to do him, too."

I knew exactly what she meant: Oz and I are what you'd call "unclockable," the kind of men most straight people would never assume would have sex with other men. But I didn't know whether to take it as a compliment or an insult since, in essence, it was both.

"Is he fuckin' you?" she directed at Oz.

"Hell no," Oz coughed up, as if she insulted him by even asking such a thing.

She turned to me; guess she knew she couldn't just accept his word for it, since he already proved himself to be a liar.

"No, I'm not," I confirmed.

I could actually see *relief* wash over her face.

"So you doin' him because I won't let you fuck me in the ass?"

"Nah."

"Then you're doin' him because you like to fuck *men* in the ass."

He hesitantly nodded yes.

She sighed. "I take it he isn't the first ... but he will be the last."

That's right; let him have it in front of his jump-off so he will be less inclined to creep in the future, knowing that he runs the risk of having you show up again.

"How many times a week?"

"Just once a week."

"'Just once a week'. As if 'just once a week' isn't one time too many."

Oz shrugged.

"How long has this been goin' on?"

"Like ... two years."

"And I take it another two years is on the agenda?"

"Actually," I interjected, "that's what we were just discussing. I told Oz that we can't see each other anymore."

"Why not?"

Hmm. That's not the response I expected. Maybe she didn't understand me ... "Things have gotten ... complicated. So, it's best that we end it."

"You can't."

Is she for real? "We ... can't?"

"That's what I said."

"Wait a minute: Are you saying you *want* us to continue seeing each other?"

"Yes, I do."

Is that what she meant by 'he will be your last'? "Why?"

"I can't control his desire. And I can't control what he does with it. A man is gonna creep. Period. If it ain't with you, it'll be with somebody else. And that's all it can be: some*body* else, not somebod*ies*."

I had to spell this out, out loud, so that *I* could make sense of it. "So ... you are OK with your husband cheating on you with a man?"

"It ain't cheating if I know about it—and approve of it."

I guess she could tell by the expression on my face that I couldn't believe what *I* was hearing.

She sat down on the sofa. "I have too much invested in Ozwald. We've known each other for 34 years, ever since we were both five, and have been married for eighteen of them. If this is what he wants so he can continue being the husband I need him to be, so be it. So long as it's just a fuck, I can deal."

Yes ... this is my out!

And Oz knew I would go there; his eyes were pleading with me not to. "Are you gonna tell her or am I?"

"Tell me what?" she demanded to know.

He struggled with the words. "I ... we ... kinda kissed."

Her eyes traveled from Oz to me, then back to Oz. "Oh?"

"More like *you* kissed *me*," I corrected him. "Tell her *why* you did it, Oz."

Oz looked in the direction of the front door; *was he going to make a run for it?* "Ilovehim," he hurried out like before.

A slight grin formed on her face. "Do you now?"

"Yeah."

"Why?"

Her response threw him. He frowned at her. "What?"

"*Why* do you love him?"

"'Cause I ... I ... I just do."

"Are you *in* love with him?"

"Uh ... uh ... I don't know."

"Well, if you don't know, that means you aren't. You would know if you were. And I have the feeling ... you don't really love him."

"Why you say that?"

"Because, if you *really* loved him, you'd be able to tell me why. Whenever someone has asked you over the years why you love me, you can rattle off a dozen or so reasons why. Clearly, Christopher doesn't have your heart—and after two years, he doesn't have what it takes to win it." She looked at me. "No offense."

"None taken," I assured her.

"So, no, I don't believe you love him. Maybe you *want* to, maybe what you have going on excites you so much that you believe it can be more than what it is—but even *I* know that is impossible. You can't turn a ho' into a housewife." Her eyes met mine. "Again, no offense."

This heifer just called me a ho'—*in my own damn house!!!* I wanted so bad to knock her teeth in but let it slide. "Again, none taken."

"Besides, there is much more at stake here than our marriage and my heart. I'm sure Ozwald doesn't want to disappoint his parents. And he most certainly wants to protect his style of life."

Protect his style of life?

She opened her purse. I eyed the pepper spray, sitting on the dining room table just inches away from my right hand.

She pulled out ... *is that what I think it is?* "OK, how much?"

It *was* what I thought it was: a check book. I couldn't believe she was taking it there ... "How much do I want for what?"

She took the cap off of a blue ball point pen. "How much do you want to keep this ... thing going?"

"I don't want your money."

"But you *do* want my husband."

"I *wanted* him. Not anymore."

"You can't put out a fire like that. Especially for a man like Ozwald. Believe me, *I* know. I am hurting—a lot right now—but I still burn for him. So you may not *want* to want him, but you still do."

Now she was trying to psychoanalyze me! The odd and very irritating thing was ... she was correct in her assessment.

"Look, he's ... stuck on you. I get that. I know he wants to continue seeing you. And I don't mind if he does."

"You don't?"

"Not that much I don't. I can deal with it. So the only thing preventing this ... thing from continuing is you. If you won't do it for him, maybe you'll do it for some cash."

I was still floored by the proposition. "So, you're willing to put your marriage in jeopardy?"

"And how would I be doing that? The cat's out of the bag, the cards are on the table. The only risk I am taking is trusting my husband will continue to see you and only you. But that's a small risk given what else could happen if you end it. He—*we*—would have to start over, and I'm not about to watch him do any comparison shopping. So as long as you don't get in *our* way, I'll stay out of *yours*."

"I ... I can't take your money."

"You said you *can't*; you didn't say you *won't*. Just name your price."

"I'm *not* for sale."

"*Everybody's* for sale. I don't see what the problem could be ... unless you're one of those interlopers that gets off being with a married man so long as the wife doesn't know."

That gave me a jolt. "Interloper?"

"Yes, interloper."

Bitch! OK, that's it ... "Alright, this has gone on long enough. *Leave*, and take your husband with you." I held the door open for her to do just that.

She rose. She glared at Oz. "Let's go."

Oz peered at me; that look silently screamed *"Save me!"* He trudged out of the apartment.

She filled out the check. She tore it off the ledger. She placed it on the end table. "Sleep on it."

I slammed the door. I picked up the check. My eyes nearly popped out of my head:

Olivia & Ozwald Johnson / Pay to the order of Christopher Nicholson / $25,000. / Twenty five thousand dollars / Memo: Marriage Counseling/One year

I'd never seen a check with five figures before in my life—and it was made out to *me*.

I slept on the check—*literally*. It rested under my pillow that night.

The next morning, I deposited it into my savings account.

FRIDAY NITE SMACKDOWN!

Thursday, June 23, 2011–9:10 pm

DJ: Welcome back to Da Spot! This is your boi, DJ Korrupt, and we are coming to the end of a very intense and interesting dialogue between two of our most prominent and revered activists, Carlton Cooke-Young and Malcolm Hightower. If you're just tuning in: what the fluck!

[Laughter]

DJ: We've been doing this roundtable during Pride month for three years now, so y'all should've known tonight was the night. We were just discussing what some have been calling an outbreak of homophobia amongst Black people: faggot being shouted by Kobe Bryant and Jaokim Noah during the past NBA season, Tracy Morgan's act in Tennessee last month, and now former NFL quarterback David Tyree saying that anarchy will ensue if same sex marriage is passed in New York.

Carlton [laughs]: Anarchy. Ridiculous.

DJ: Just before the break, Carlton, who you just heard, was reading David the riot act for the PSA he did for the National Organization for Marriage. Malcolm, you wanted to respond?

Malcolm: You know I do. And thanks for not saying, quote, the f-word, end quote.

DJ: You know we don't use code on this show, brutha!

Malcolm: And I respect and love you for it. I don't have a problem with homophobes being called out. But, once again, a brutha is made the example, is the scapegoat, is tagged as *the* face of homophobia. It's one thing to challenge Kobe, Jaokim, Tracy and David on why what they said is toxic; it's another to tar and feather them, to call on the torch bearers and lynch mob, to act as if this is the first time anyone has said such things—or that their saying it is worse *because* they are Black.

Carlton: I didn't say that it's worse; I said they should know better *because* they are black.

Malcolm: Same coin, different side.

Carlton: No, it's not.

Malcolm: How is it not? You are holding them to a different standard because they have melanin that you don't hold others to—those others, of course, being white people. As if having melanin means someone has to fall lock in step with whatever agenda the caucasian queer community pushes.

Carlton: How is equality for all LGBTQ people an agenda of the caucasian queer community? Black and other ethnic minorities who also happen to be LGBTQ will benefit from DADT and DOMA being repealed, and ENDA being passed.

Malcolm: It's not about the agenda not benefiting us; it's about the agenda being set by them and their believing we're supposed to just sign on. They expect Black SGL people to just go along with the agenda *they* plan, and Black heteros to understand and champion the cause because *they* allegedly marched on Washington in 1963. What ever. And when's the *first* time a white homophobe was forced to go on an apology tour like Tracy? You'd think Tracy would've learned from Isaiah.

DJ: Washington?

Malcolm: Right. Look how they crucified that brutha. He went on CNN and apologized, and the white gay mafia in Follywood *still* whiteballed his ass.

DJ: Whiteballed. I like that.

Malcolm: And who is GLAAD to demand an apology from anyone? Who do they represent? Certainly not Black SGL folk.

Carlton: Would you be saying that if Tracy agreed to meet with *your* group?

Malcolm: Tracy probably doesn't even know my group exists. But if he *did* meet with us, we wouldn't parade him in public to embarrass and emasculate him.

Carlton: Emasculate?

Malcolm: Yes, emasculate. The whole episode was amped up to make him kowtow. Like with Isaiah, GLAAD's whole approach was: "Bad nigger! Bad, bad, nigger! Now you're gonna get a public flogging!" And, as they showed with Isaiah, GLAAD isn't interested in opening up and having an authentic, continuous dialogue about homophobia in Black communities. Who is the main target of homophobia from Black folks? *We* are. Yet you'd never know that, since the representatives of the so-called gay community sitting across the table from the offenders during episodes like this are *never* Black.

DJ: Well, in this case, Tracy did meet with at least one Black SGL person publicly, but even that was problematic for me. Jayden Love, the young man from the Ali Forney Center, really brought the issue home. It's rare that SGL youth of color are granted a microphone to tell their story. I had him and a couple of other younger folks on the show in March. But ... there was something about that meeting that rubbed me the wrong way. It felt like he was being exploited to help Tracy repair his image and so GLAAD could one-up HRC as *the* premiere gay spokesgroup. Is that even a word?

[Laughter]

Malcolm: It is now, and I agree with you, one hundred.

DJ: It reminded me of Tim Hardaway and his visit to a gay youth center after his "I hate gay people" rant. It came off kind of forced and fake. What are your thoughts on that, Carlton?

Carlton: Well, I don't think it's fair to fault GLAAD for doing what its mission states: fighting defamation against gay and lesbian people. Now, we may not always like the methods they use to do it or the approach they take, but they can't be all things to all people.

Malcolm: Obviously.

Carlton: I thought Tracy visiting the Ali Forney Center turned a negative into a positive. It became a teachable moment.

Malcolm: Teachable for *who*?

Carlton: If not for Tracy, there were many other people watching, who may now get it. Even in the context of a comedy routine, there are some things that just aren't funny—and given the rash of gay teen suicides lately, that was the wrong thing for him to joke about. And, at least his apology *seemed* sincere; he didn't say "I'm sorry *if* what I said offended you."

Malcolm: But it's still not clear exactly *why* Tracy apologized. Was it *what* he said? *How* he said it? *Where* he said it? Some combination of all of the above?

DJ: Malcolm, do you believe Tracy should have apologized?

Malcolm: No, I don't. If you're gonna open your mouth and vomit, own it; other folks shouldn't have to force you to clean it up. The real issue is often overlooked: *why* they said it, the societal indifference towards and contempt for SGL people that we all have been impacted by. The whole celebrities-apologizing-for-hurting-the-feelings-of-X-group shtick is wack: They say something offensive, are called on it, issue a non-apology apology and then magically become an ally of the offended group? It's just bad theater. If *anyone* deserved an apology, it's Tracy's son—not only for being put up in that moronic mix, but for having a father who is a talentless hack.

DJ [chuckles]: Yeah, Tracy has seriously gotten over. He is *so* unfunny.

Malcolm: And, besides, Dan Savage, the caucasian queer community's super-spokesperson, *still* hasn't apologized for his racist trip in '08, nor have any of those caucasian queer groups in Cali that spearheaded the failed No on Prop 8 campaign that discounted the contributions and ignored the voices of SGL people of color.

Carlton: Not that they *shouldn't* ... but what if any of those entities *did* apologize? You'd still say that wasn't enough.

Malcolm: Of course I would because it *wouldn't* be enough. What's so hard about being proactive in your advocacy? Don't get upset with me because I point out the systemic exclusion of people of color and their hypocrisy in not dealing with it—*do* something about it. Because these incidents get turned into publicity stunts, the right dialogue doesn't take place and the true lessons folks can learn aren't. Which is why GLAAD should've just stayed out of it; in the end, they bullied Tracy, just like Tim and Isaiah, into taking a stand so that they could do what they do best: grandstand.

Carlton: *GLAAD* bullied *them*? Are you saying they should've been given a pass because they are black?

Malcolm: You did *not* hear that come out of my mouth.

Carlton: I'm just trying to get clarity.

Malcolm: No, you're just trying to get *crafty*.

Carlton: Crafty?

Malcolm: Yeah, *crafty*. Just because I want the same rules of engagement to be applied with Black folks who display homophobic/heterosexist tendencies that are employed with everyone else does *not* mean I believe they should get a pass.

Carlton: If someone white said the same things they did, they'd also be raked over the coals.

Malcolm: Probably, but none of these caucasian queers would be harping on their *lack* of melanin as a point of attack. I don't want to send any of your listeners to the caucasian queer websites or blogs in question, but no sooner than the items about Kobe, Jaokim, Tracy and David went up, you'd think you were reading Stormfront or Free Republic, just in queerface. The white hoods came out and nigger was tossed around like a football—just like when Prop 8 passed and they decided we were to blame. "How dare *they* vote against *us!*" As if we owe them something. As if they own our votes. As if they own *us*. There is a nuance that is often missing when the topic is homophobia and the people in question are Black. In fact, they've come up with a special, racist name for it: black homophobia.

DJ: Hmm. Educate me, brutha: why is the descriptor *black homophobia* racist?

Malcolm: Notice that the bile spewed by the likes of Maggie Gallagher, Brian Brown, Bryan Fischer or Tony Perkins isn't dubbed *white* homophobia. Why is that? Are we to assume that their whiteness doesn't impact and influence how they view SGL people? Of course we are, since white folks are just *individuals*. You never hear, "The *white* community is virulently homophobic"—even though there is *plenty* of evidence to back up that statement. Who runs the Christianist, Roman Catholic, and Mormon Churches, which bankroll the anti-gay industry? Who heads all those think-of-the-children anti-family groups, and pickets the funerals of dead soldiers with "God Hates Fags" signs? And, who crafted and cast the majority of the votes that passed Prop 8 and every other anti-gay amendment or proposition in the country? The white parents, grandparents, siblings, and other relatives of *caucasian queer* folks. But *they* get the benefit of the doubt—and why shouldn't they, since not all white people are the same and, as such, not all white homophobes are the same. Age, family dynamics, educational background, and one's social, political, cultural, and religious stations must be considered and contextualized in order to challenge their ignorance and change their hearts, change their minds, and change the laws. Not the case with us. We are, quote, *the black community*, end quote, this conspiratorial mass of monolithic bigots that is threatening the caucasian queer way of life. Even the terminology used against us is melodramatic and denotes pathology. Our homophobia isn't just a problem: it's *running rampant*, it's *raging*, it's *notorious*, it's *vicious*, it's *insidious*. And the word you used earlier: "There is an *outbreak* ..." What, do Black people catch and spread homophobia like the flu?

[DJ laughs]

Malcolm: Three Black folks say something homophobic and *we're* having the most homophobic month ever? How many white public figures said homophobic crap in the same month? Thirty? Three hundred? With us, the narrative is never "*X* is a homophobe"; it's always, "*The black community* is homophobic." When *one* Black person says something stupid, *all* Black people are held responsible for it.

Carlton: No one expects *all* black people to answer for the homophobic words or deeds of one black person.

Malcolm [chuckles]: You livin' in the same country I am?

Carlton: Look, there's a difference between viewing all black people with contempt and holding those black people in contempt who are bigots. And since African Americans have been through hell trying to secure our own rights and rightful place in this country—and, yes, as much as you try to dismiss it, some white gays and lesbians stood with us back then and stand with us today in fighting racial injustice—

Malcolm: Right. *Some.* Not *many.* Not *most. Some.*

Carlton:—it's hard not to notice when black heterosexuals spew the kind of hate that would make David Duke smile. There was a time when blacks couldn't marry *each other*, so how can a group with that kind of history support any kind of legislation that denies marriage equality and other rights to another minority group? It's a visceral and natural reaction.

Malcolm: Well, it shouldn't be. Caucasian queers do not nail Maggie Gallagher to the cross for forgetting the suffrage and feminist movements. Nor do they blast *each other* for expressing racist views—shouldn't *they* know better since they are gay and know what it's like to face bigotry? Again, it's a double standard, they are not being consistent. Fact: Black folks—like any other people—can be homophobic. Caucasian queers need to deal with it, accept it, and get over it and their pollyanish/we are the world/let's all wave a rainbow flag expectation that the Negroes are *supposed* to automatically empathize with and embrace the gay rights fight. It's lazy, self-righteous, patronizing, and puts a very ugly spotlight on their entitlement issues. You don't get to dictate or police the opinions or actions of Black folks; we don't need your permission to be anything—and that, unfortunately, includes being bigots. It's something *all* humans can be, but that's the kicker: Many of those harping on so-called black homophobia don't see Black people as *human*. And, as Jayden and the stories of too many other Black SGL people highlight, there are Black folks who won't accept their own SGL children, who have kicked them out of the house, disowned them; what makes them [white gays and lesbians] think these *same* folks will support something like same sex marriage? Talk about white supremacist arrogance.

Carlton: Oh, come on. White supremacist arrogance?

Malcolm: Yes. Don't you, the gay black man married to the so-called anti-racist caucasian queer activist, know what that is?

Carlton: Again, Josh is not a part of this conversation.

Malcolm: If he was, I'm sure he'd explain that the white folks in question are so blinded by their white skin privilege that they fail to recognize that there are Black people on this earth who are also SGL. They will, in the same breath, claim that Black people are more homophobic *and* that caucasian queers are less racist. Like they actually know Black people. Like they actually *care* about Black people—including the SGL ones. They don't. They do not have the authority to lecture any of us about racism *or* homophobia, about the similarities or parallels between the two forms of bigotry, or to misappropriate the separate but equal hallmarks of white supremacy and presume that gay is the new black. And just because we have the Civil Rights Act of 1964, the Voting Rights Act of 1965, affirmative action, *The Cosby Show*, Oprah, Denzel, Will, and President Obama does *not* mean that we have overcome. The Freedom Movement hasn't ended: We're *still* going through hell. Hello, Jena 6? Sean Bell? Mitrice Richardson? Oscar Grant? My own father went to a colored elementary school in Montgomery, Alabama; *his* father was lynched by the KKK. That wasn't that long ago.

Carlton: But you have to acknowledge that the vestiges of Jim Crow are gone.

Malcolm: *Are* they?

Carlton: Of course they are! Do you see "Whites Only" signs on bathrooms and water fountains, or "Colored" sections of buses and trains? As Wanda Sykes pointed out, there isn't a NOM, an American Family Association, or a Family Research Council pushing and passing legislation or ordinances to block black people's access or mobility as full-fledged citizens.

Malcolm: With all due respect, they *are* pushing and passing legislation and ordinances to block the access and mobility of Black people—Black *SGL* people. Remember that

Tony Perkins and David Duke are cut from the same white hooded cloths; Tony has spoken in front of white supremacist groups and even purchased the KKK's phone bank from a Grand Wizard. And, white supremacy is so endemic, so entrenched in the psyche and fabric of this society it doesn't *need* to be pushed by any one group—although too many of *us* aid and abet it. It's not a coincidence that a Black man with an undergraduate degree earns, on average, the same amount of green as a white man with a high school diploma. Or that a Black man has a better chance of being incarcerated than matriculated. Or that Black women account for the majority of discharges under Don't Ask, Don't Tell. Or that the faces propped up as the most important in the so-called gay rights movement are caucasian—and the faces often branded the most homophobic are Black. Just because the "Whites Only" signs can no longer be displayed doesn't mean the "Whites Only"—and, by extension, "White is right"—mentality has died. The racism is just remixed and shelled out differently. Jim Crow didn't die; he just got a makeover.

DJ: Tell it, Malcolm—you are comin' *hard*!

Carlton: Well, I wish he would also come hard against black ho-, uh, black people who are homophobic the way he does white gays and lesbians who are racist.

Malcolm: If anything, I come down harder on *us*.

Carlton: Not from what I've heard.

Malcolm: That's because this is the only Black-identified space you can be bothered with.

Carlton [sighs]: What does that mean?

Malcolm: That means you're not in the trenches every-day, like I am. The barbershops, the beauty shops, the b-ball courts, the churches, hosting community forums with Reverend Al Sharpton and the National Action Network. You ain't gonna see or hear those types of dialogues on the shows you've appeared on: Anderson Cooper, Rachel Maddow, Michelangelo Signorile, Keith Olbermann. The truth is, my calling out white folks makes you uncomfortable because you work with a white-identified group.

Carlton [laughs]: Why must you make everything personal when talking politics?

Malcolm: I don't. But *you* opened that door. Besides, the personal *is* political.

DJ: Let's end this discussion on a positive note. At least I hope we can with this final topic: Don Lemon's coming out. Right now, he is the country's most high profile openly gay Black man, coming into millions of homes each day. Any thoughts on his announcement and what, if anything, it does or can mean for Black SGL people?

Malcolm: His profile is not as large but let's not forget Will Sheridan, the former Villanova U starter. His making it official will mean much more than Don's, in the long run.

DJ: Why do you say that?

Malcolm: Because, Don is very much detached from Black people.

Carlton: How do you know that? Are you sleeping with him?

Malcolm: Ha, now even *you* know that ain't possible. [chuckles]

Carlton: Just because he is partnered with a white man means he's detached from black people ... ?

Malcolm: No. But expecting other Black SGL men to want to be partnered with white men, to beat down the doors of caucasian queer folks that don't want to include us? Yes, that makes him detached. It's also the way he talks about Black folks: Being on the so-called down low is *more prevalent* and *worse* in the so-called black community?

DJ: Yeah, the hair on the back of my neck stood up when he said that.

Malcolm: And it should have. As if there is something more sinister about Black men—and let's not forget the sisters—leading closeted lives? What ever.

Carlton: I don't want to speak for him, but I believe he meant that, as you yourself say, there is a *peculiar* don't ask, don't tell policy in place that prevents many of us from even broaching the subject—which leads to more of us being closeted. The fact that there are so few out black celebrities is proof of that.

Malcolm: *If* that's what he meant, *that's* what he should have said. The phrase down low shouldn't have been a part of the conversation. What was once a benign identifier used by bruthaz in the late eighties and early nineties who didn't embrace any of the alphabet soup labels but moved in circles with men who did has become a pejorative to tag not just those who are undercover but *all* Black SGL men. And now, a decade in, that single media-manipulated phrase continues to taint any healthy dialogue and block transformative movement surrounding homophobia in Black America. Like too many, Don's fallen for the hype. Even he himself admitted he didn't really know about the DL, yet he feels he has the experience and authority to make ill-informed statements about it? Why would he parrot that racist, homophobic narrative? Also, I know somebody is not gonna like *this* ...

Carlton: Well, you're looking directly at me so it's clear who you're referring to.

Malcolm: ... but Don was moved to finally take that step because a white boy jumped off a bridge.

Carlton [sighs]: You are *actually* spitting on Tyler Clementi's grave.

Malcolm: I am not. I'm just pointing out that the suicides of Raymond Chase and Joseph Jefferson, the executions of Lawrence King and August Provost, the murder and dismemberment of Rashawn Brazell, and the bullycides of Carl Joseph Walker-Hoover and Jaheem Herrera are just as worthy of being recognized and remembered. Don clearly sees being gay through a prism of whiteness, and that has worked out for him. But is that what we want young bruthaz to embrace and emulate, that the lives of caucasian queer men have more value than their own? I don't think so.

Carlton: So, because Tyler's story touched him, that means he believes a white man's life is worth more? You can't decide how or why a person comes to terms with who they are, what event will change their life and encourage them to take that new path. I'm glad Don was so moved by Tyler's story that it finally pushed him to publicly reveal what many already knew because that will mean one less soul lost, one less boy or girl believing that it doesn't get better. They can point to another gay person who came through his own trials and is well-adjusted, sophisticated, and accomplished. In the end it doesn't matter *how* he got there, just that he did.

DJ: Malcolm, how do you think Will's being out will have more impact than Don's, in the long run?

Malcolm: Because of his age; it helps when that public figure is a part of or close to your peer group. And, besides being a b-baller, he's a rapper. A boi in the 'hood struggling with his sexual identity will definitely relate.

Carlton: A boy in the 'hood can't also relate to Don ... ?

Malcolm: I'm sure some can. But, for most young Black men in the 'hood, one's masculinity, one's social identity is often tied to sports and hip-hop. And it's rare when you can point to a public figure who is in both worlds *and* is also SGL.

DJ: You may not agree on whose coming out is or will be more significant, but I'm sure you both can agree that the journeys of both men illustrate that Black SGL people are indeed everywhere, everything, and everyone.

Malcolm and Carlton: Yeah.

DJ: And on that note, we have to wrap things up. But if you're in New York, you can still catch my guests at different events this weekend. Carlton will be honored at the Empire State Pride Agenda's annual banquet tomorrow night, as one of their Emerging Activists Under 30. He just made the cut at 29. Congrats, again, man.

Carlton: Thanks.

DJ: And you will be marching in Sunday's parade?

Carlton: Yes. With the Color Blind Queers contingent.

DJ: With Josh?

Carlton: Yes. He'll be making his way to New York Saturday afternoon.

DJ: And Malcolm and his group, the Bruthahood, will have a booth at Harlem Pride on Saturday. What time will you be there again?

Malcolm: From two to four.

DJ: And you're also having a mixer later that night, from six to eight, at Hue-Man Bookstore.

Malcolm: Yup. Our special guests will be best-selling author Mitchell Crawford and award-winning actor Raheim Rivers.

DJ: Ah man! Talk about a super role model couple! *They* should be grand marshals of the Pride parade.

Malcolm: Ha, now you know that ain't *never* happenin'. Too much melanin in the mix.

DJ: Had them both on the show a couple of years ago, and Mitchell this past February to promote his new book, *You Can't Always Want What You Get.* I will most definitely be popping by there.

Malcolm: Look forward to seeing you, brutha.

DJ: Thanks again, gents. It was another hot one! Same time, next year?

Malcolm: You know it.

Carlton: Wouldn't miss it for the world.

DJ: Cool. Thanks for tuning in, folks. If you missed any of tonight's show or any other episodes, just go to www.DaSpot.com or hit us up on Facebook. You can also get more info on our guests. Hope to see many of you out this weekend; Da Spot will also have a booth at Harlem Pride, so if you see us stop on by. Happy Pride!

Friday, June 24, 2011–11:57 p.m.

"Congratulations."
Carlton was waiting on an elevator in the lobby of the Marriott Marquis in mid-town, where he was staying for the weekend and the Empire State Pride Agenda was hosting their banquet. After having drinks and chatting with a few of the special guests, such as Kathy Griffin and Russell Simmons, he decided to call it a night.

He recognized the voice immediately—and it was the last one he wanted to hear, especially on such an important evening. Not only was his award presented to him by John Amaechi, but the attendees received the historic news that marriage equality had just passed in the New York Senate.

"What are you doing here?" snapped Carlton, not looking in his direction.

"Usually people say 'Thank you' when someone congratulates them."

The elevator door opened. Carlton got on; Malcolm followed. Carlton pressed the button for the sixth floor. The door closed. They stood on opposite sides.

"Your acceptance speech is already posted on YouTube," Malcolm informed him.

Carlton's eyes stayed fixed on the floor counter, which displayed the numbers in red.

"It was good."

Floor "5" flashed.

"A brutha pays you a compliment and you have nothing to say?"

The elevator door opened. Carlton exited with Malcolm on his heels.

"*Loved* how you threw that growing up in the ghetto line in there. That always goes over well with the white liberal crowd."

Carlton stopped. His head whipped around to the right. "What would *you* know about the ghetto? *You* didn't grow up in one."

"Yeah, I grew up in Baldwin Hills, and I'm not ashamed of that. *You*, on the other hand, haven't set foot in South Central in years. It must be *so* hard, tearing yourself away from that tony townhouse in Boystown you reside in as the kept boy of a trust fund brat old enough to be your father."

Carlton grinned. "And you wish you were in my shoes."

Malcolm chuckled. "You must be drunk."

Carlton was a little light-headed but nowhere near drunk. He moved in, eyeballing Malcolm. "One doesn't have to be drunk to see the jealousy in those not-so-green eyes of yours."

Malcolm returned the stare-down; they were now nose to nose. At six feet, he was three inches taller than Carlton. "You forget that I don't do windows, women or white boys?"

"That's what you say. But given the chance—and the right price—you would."

"We know what *your* price was—and you came real cheap."

Carlton snickered. "*Cheap?* You shouldn't talk about *cheap.* I'm not the one standing here in an Old Navy tank, Kmart cargo shorts, and Payless sandals."

"I'm not a label ho'—like you."

"But you *are* a fake-ass poser."

"*'Fake-ass poser'?* Is that another niggaism you heard from your wish-he-could-out-Black-the-Black-folks husband?"

"Huh, he sure as hell can out-black *you.*"

"Only in *your* colonized mind. I'm surprised he let you off the plantation for the weekend. But I see the shackle is still on." Malcolm's left index finger brushed the right side of Carlton's neck.

Carlton swatted his hand away. "Don't *fuckin'* put your hands on me."

Malcolm moved forward, bumping Carlton's shoulders with his chest. He wasn't muscular like Carlton, but did have a stocky frame.

"And don't *fuckin'* push up on me," Carlton snapped.

Malcolm giggled. "You on a roll tonight. *'Push up'?* You must've gotten *that* one from a rerun of *Living Single.*"

Malcolm pushed forward again, this time harder, knocking Carlton into his room door. Carlton's arms flew up. Malcolm grabbed his wrists. They tangled and wrangled, scuffled and tussled until ...

... Malcolm aimed for and caught Carlton's lips with his own. Carlton continued to struggle, mouthing *"What the fuck? You fuckin' crazy?"* through their lip lock. But then ... he *tasted* Malcolm. *Mmm ... like butter almond with a caramel swirl.* His favorite ice cream. Carlton stopped fighting and totally surrendered to the kiss. His arms found their way around and locked in a fold behind Malcolm's neck.

Malcolm was into it, too—*Yeah, I'm gettin' me some of this mocha chocolata ya ya tonite*—but not *that* into it that he didn't know it was up to him to slip Carlton's room key out of his left hand and insert it in the door. Malcolm pushed down the door handle and, with his left arm around Carlton's waist, pushed them into the room, the door closing behind them.

And that's when the fight—uh, the fuck—broke out.

They crashed into the desk with such force that the telephone receiver was knocked off its base and onto the floor. Good thing the reading lamp was screwed to the desk or it might've suffered a similar fate.

Malcolm kicked the trash pail out of his way, sending it flying across the room and onto the queen-sized bed. Carlton grazed the framed watercolor painting on the wall with his right shoulder, causing it to tilt to the left.

The way Malcolm gripped and squeezed Carlton, you'd think he was a boa constrictor.

The way Carlton clenched and scratched Malcolm's short 'fro, you'd think he was trying to scalp him.

Malcolm lifted Carlton and dropped him on the dresser, making the attached mirror shake.

Malcolm unzipped his fly and pulled out his very fat, long dick.

Carlton kicked off his flip-flops (which also landed on the bed), slid off his white trousers and white g-string and tossed them onto the tv set (surprisingly, his iPhone didn't fall out his back pocket), and pulled his knees into his chest to reveal that plum ass hole, a-twitchin'.

Smiling at the very inviting canal he planned to occupy, Malcolm shoved his very thick, left middle finger inside.

"*Ooohoohooh,*" Carlton yelped.

"*Yeah,*" Malcolm answered, shoving harder and digging deeper.

As he continued to finger fuck Carlton, Malcolm pulled a gold, square packet out of his back pocket, ripped it open with his teeth, and rolled the condom down on his dick.

"You ready for this?" Malcolm wondered out loud, admiring his own dick as his finger still played hide and seek in Carlton's ass.

"Get the fuck up in it and you'll find out," Carlton snarled.

Malcolm jammed the dick inside. "*Aw yeah!* That's what I'm talkin' 'bout! You nice 'n' tight. You ain't *never* felt it like this, huh? See what happens when you hook up with the white boy—you miss out on good shit like *this*! I *know* he can't put it on ya like *me*!"

All the noise annoyed Carlton—and was killing the groove he was trying to establish. So Carlton smacked Malcolm upside his head, *hard*. "Ezra, will you just shut your verbose ass the *fuck* up and let your cock do the talkin'!"

Malcolm was horrified—but not because Carlton had the gall to call him by his first name, which he hates. "*Cock?* I ain't got no *cock*, mutha-fucka. I got a *dick*."

"Like there's a difference?"

"Hell-fuckin' yeah. And you about to *feel* it." Malcolm began employing his special slide to the side stroke that, legend has it, makes all the boiz hoot and holler.

All the boiz *except* Carlton, that is.

While Malcolm had shut off the yak, he still wore that *My shit don't stink-I'm always right you're always wrong* grin he usually flashes when they are on the air or in public debating. He loved to hear himself talk, and clearly loved to watch himself fuck: for three minutes, his eyes never veered away from his own profile in the mirror.

It was Carlton's turn to talk shit.

"Hell-o? Is this fuckin' thing on? Come on, that *all* you got? That *all* you workin' with? That *all* you comin' with? *Fuck!* You got all that ... *dick,* and don't know what to do with it? I may as well be with the white boy. He got better motion for this ocean. Looks like he *can* really out-black you!" Carlton let out a maniacal laugh.

Now ... why would he wanna say *that?*

Of course, this made Malcolm *mad*—and he took it out on the ass.

Malcolm ejected his dick. He snatched Carlton up by his unbuttoned white shirt (causing it to rip and a few of the buttons to pop off), flung him around, and threw him back down. Carlton knew *just* what to do: He separated his knees as far as he could, arched his back inward, and tooted the ass *up.* Malcolm dove right on down—and *drove* that dick in him as if he were competing in the Indianapolis 500.

And did that make Carlton *ever* so glad: He planted both hands on the mirror and twirled and swirled his hips, right on the upstroke and left on the down. Every poke made not only the dresser rock but the bed (which was at least ten feet away and leaning against the *opposite* wall) knock.

For a sweat-drenching fifteen minutes, the only sounds were the dresser bouncing up and down with the bed providing an echo, the decorative prongs on top of the mirror digging into the wall and causing paint and plaster to fall, Malcolm punching Carlton's cheeks with both clenched fists, and Carlton's "Oh, fuck ... " being answered with Malcolm's "Ah shit ... "

Then Carlton's "Oh, fuck!" with Malcolm's "Ah shit!"

Then Carlton's *"Oh, fuck!"* with Malcolm's *"Ah shit!"*

Then Carlton's final *"Oh, fuuuuck!"* with Malcolm's final *"Ah sheeee-iiiit!"*

As the painting finally fell and landed face-down, they both blew it—Carlton all over the mirror and Malcolm all over Carlton's ass and his shirt.

After squeezing out the last of his juice, Malcolm shook his dick a few times and stuffed it back in his shorts.

Carlton spread his cheeks, allowing his hot hole to cool off. Despite all the smudges and dozens of fingerprints, he caught Malcolm's eye in the mirror. "You're *still* an arrogant, pompous, self-important, self-absorbed, wannabe Malcolm X agitator."

"You're *still* an Oreo dipped, stuck-up, corporate suck-up, gaystream mouthpiece and apologist for your caucasian queer Massas," Malcolm shot back.

They *stared* for a few seconds.

"Same time, next year?" Carlton whispered.

"You know it," Malcolm winked. He exited the room, the door closing behind him.

Carlton fingered his very hot hole, grinning. "Wouldn't miss it for the world."

CAN YOU FEEL WHAT I'M SAYING?

Ellington was waiting. A man like him is always wait-ing—at least that's what most (if not all) seeing people believe. Those "vision impaired," those "pupil-challenged," those "eyeless " (as he overheard one woman say to another) folk are all waiting on the world to help them. To protect them. To coddle them. To have pity on them. To have sympathy for them. To *see* them.

Ellington wasn't that kind of blind man, and he knew most seeing people didn't really see *him*. They only saw a fig-ure they *wanted* to help, to protect, to coddle, to pity, or to have sympathy for—as if he wanted it, needed it, or asked for it. He learned some time ago that those people could only rec-ognize him if his existence affirmed or confirmed their feel-ings, their idea of what a blind man is or should be.

But today he was waiting. For the first time, waiting. On one of those people. And he didn't mind.

Sure, he was going to be a few minutes late. And yes, there were a few people who offered to guide him across the street. But his day wouldn't be the same without him.

The walk from the 23rd Street station on the F Line to his office is ninety nine steps. He'd been making this trek for almost five years but only began enjoying it fourteen months ago. Yes, he was pleased to have a position that actually uti-lized his talents and didn't stick him in a corner for seven hours with nothing to do but fill some Americans with Dis-abilities Act quota, as was the case with his first two jobs out of college. And he loved the work; it was his life's work. Not many can say they are doing what they love to do and earn a more than respectable salary doing it. He was thankful. Always thankful. He was taught to be (well, *told* to be). Thankful that he could see the first eight years of his life. That he had the kind of family that wouldn't allow him to become dependent on them or the outside world. That he didn't have to pay a dime for that "special school," or his four years at Fordham University, or the first year's rent on his first apartment. That he had a rather active social life and even managed to date.

But he was even more thankful, *most* thankful when the Lord brought this man into his life. And to think they had been riding the same train for three years and hadn't known it.

At least Ellington never knew it. Ellington rode in the fourth car of the train, where he could make his exit through the last door, walk eight steps and go through the second turstyle, turn left, walk twelve steps, go up the stairwell (twenty six steps), then four steps to the northeast corner of 23rd Street. Antwan rode the first car. It's possible that Antwan had seen him before, or noticed him but was in too much of a hurry to stop and offer assistance. But Ellington doubts it. A man like Antwan wouldn't have. And if he had, Ellington would have known for he never could have forgotten that smell. Ellington could always … well, *sniff* Antwan out as he approached. Before he spoke or touched him, he took him *in*. He's never asked what the smell is. He's afraid that if he did, he wouldn't smell the same again. A fragrance doesn't sit on the skin or permeate the pores the same way on everyone, and that has everything to do with the type of energy they give off, the spirit they exude, even the clothes they're wearing, the kind of day they're having, whether they got enough sleep the night before, or got some. Ellington had no idea what the aroma was but was sure that, even if it was a fashionable brand, no one else could wear it like Antwan. The smell alone gave him a woody.

Ellington wondered: *Has Antwan noticed how I smell?* Not that he smells any particular way, since he doesn't wear cologne. Or, more importantly, *Has he noticed that I've been clinging to him a little closer, gripping him a little tighter, holding on to him a little longer each morning?* He *had* to. A man knows when a man is getting next to him—especially one who doesn't like other men getting next to him. Antwan has never flinched or recoiled, but that doesn't necessarily mean he wants to or likes to get next to another man. Or, more specifically, Ellington.

But Ellington planned on finding out today.

Ellington could hear him coming, even with all the other footsteps around him. Antwan's gait was so deliberate, so stylish, so musical. Each foot firmly made contact with the ground, while the cuff of both heels tapped a beat on the up swing. *Bum bump. Bum bump. Bum bump.*

"Mornin', man," Antwan greeted, lightly slapping Ellington's upper back with his left hand.

"That it is." *Especially now that you've arrived.*

"Surprised to see you here. Nobody helped you out?"

No one has to; I know this path by heart. "Nope."

"Well, put ya hook in me."

Boy, would I love to ...

Ellington used to just clutch him around the elbow; over the past few months, he's slowly moved up to the bicep and leans on him a little harder.

The light changed; Ellington followed his lead.

"Antwan?"

"Yeah?"

"I have something to ask you."

"Shoot."

"Uh, I was wondering if ... well, my birthday is this Saturday ... "

"I know. You gonna have a party?"

"Well, in a way, yeah."

"Cool, man. Ya can't let ya thirtieth just be another day. I'm already plannin' mine and it ain't for another six months."

"I know."

"So what time is this party?"

"It starts at eight."

"You want me to bring somethin'?"

He knew he'd be invited—and I'm glad he wanted to come. "Just you."

"How many folks comin'?"

"Just you."

They were now across the street. They were facing each other.

"Man, how you gonna have a party wit' one guest?" Antwan was clueless.

"Well ... *you* would be the party. I ... I was wondering if ... if I could have you."

Ellington knew that his request might be shocking. But did the man stop breathing?

Finally, after what seemed like forever (it was actually fifteen seconds) ... "Man, that's dangerous." He sounded somewhat exasperated.

"What is?"

"Comin' at me like that."

"How is it dangerous?"

"I mighta been offended. And pounded you."

"Might've been. So, you weren't offended ... ?"

"Uh ... nah."

"Flattered?"

"Uh ... yeah."

Ellington had never attempted a cartwheel before, but he felt like doing one then.

"And how would you explain to the police and dozens of witnesses that a *blind* man was hitting on you, so you beat him up?" Ellington added.

There was that laugh, rolling up from Antwan's gut and shooting out of his mouth, as if he were speaking through a megaphone.

"Uh ... how could you tell?" Antwan inquired.

"In all the time we've been crossing the street, you've never mentioned a girlfriend. In fact, you've never mentioned a woman. So, you have a boyfriend. Or just broke up with him. Or you're dating. Or you're flying solo. I'm hoping it's the last one, but a man like you ... you must be involved with someone. *Somehow.*"

"Uh, nah, not right now. But ... you attracted to *me?*"

"Yes, I'm attracted to you. You sound surprised."

"Well ... uh ... "

"*How* can I be attracted to you?"

"Yeah."

"Easy. I'm not attracted to your body, although I can feel you've been going through a transformation. A *nice* transformation."

Antwan blushed.

"You're blushing, aren't you?"

"Man, how you know?"

"Just a guess. But, how could I *not* be attracted to you? You're a great conversationalist. A great listener. You have such a hearty laugh. You're compassionate, and giving. And you've got such a sweet disposition. Warm like the oven in my mama's kitchen."

Antwan recognized the lyric and the artist who wrote and performed it immediately. "Phoebe Snow."

"Heard you listening to her on your iPod last week. Haven't come across many brothers who like her. I do, too."

"Uh, how you know I'm a brutha?"

"Come on: I may be blind but I'm not stupid. Besides, how many white men do you know named *Antwan?*"

He laughed again. Ellington's heart raced a little faster.

"Look, I know I'm just springing this on you. You don't have to give me an answer right now. Just think about it. If you say no, I'll understand. I just want to spend my special day ... well, *night*, with someone special."

"Uh, a'ight, man. I'll ... think about it. I better get to work. Have a good day."

"Thanks. You, too. Same time tomorrow?"

"Yeah."

Although Antwan seemed to respond to the overture well, Ellington had the feeling he wouldn't be seeing him the same time tomorrow. And he was right: Instead of the four minutes he waited the day before, he stood at the corner for ten. He was not only disappointed, he was disappointed *in* Antwan. Even if the answer was no (and it evidently was) he knew Antwan would have the integrity and decency to tell him in person. He was crushed, *by* his crush.

Ellington was a few steps away from reaching the other side of the street when he caught a *whiff*, heard the *bum bump bum bump bum bump*, and that left hand found Ellington's back.

"Man, you ain't gonna believe this ... "

You're right, I won't.

" ... but I overslept."

He couldn't come up with something a little more creative?

"I was up most of the nite ... "

Thinking of ways to let me down easy, right?

" ... thinkin' 'bout ... the party."

Oh?

"Uh ... it's still jumpin' off at eight?"

Ellington's head, which hung a little low, lifted. "Yes."

"Cool. Just gimme the address and the digits."

Ellington did. Antwan filed it in his cell.

"You sure you don't want me to bring somethin'?"

"Just yourself."

"You got some Phoebe Snow?"

"Everything she's ever recorded."

"Nice. Tomorrow nite, then."

"Great."

They usually hugged on a Friday, sort of a weekend good-bye—and today was no exception. They both knew, though, that this hug would be different from all the rest.

Antwan shook his hand, pulled him closer, drew him in with his left arm (which draped Ellington's neck), his upper chest making contact with Ellington's. Ellington roped his arm just below his shoulders.

But, unlike all the other times, Antwan didn't pull back first.

The dinner dishes were soaking (only a few tablespoons of both the wild rice and green beans were left; Ellington got a woody listening to Antwan tear into the smoked turkey breast). Their half eaten slices of the chocolate yellow layer birthday cake were on the coffee table. "Touch Your Soul" by Phoebe was playing in the background. The lights were dimmed. They were on the sofa, inches apart, turned inwards, Ellington's left knee pressed against Antwan's right. Antwan opened the bottle of champagne (which he brought); he filled their glasses. They raised them.

"Happy birthday, man. Here's to 30. And another 30. And another."

"Thanks. And here's to you."

"To me?"

"Yes. For helping make this such a special night for me."

Clink.

"So ... " Ellington began. "Why did you accept my invite?"

"Why?"

"Yes."

"I ... I can be totally honest?"

"I wouldn't want you to be anything but."

"Well ... I been feelin' you."

"Oh? For how long?"

"Like four months."

"What were or are you feeling?"

"You cool peeps. And ... I wanna get to know you better. A whole lot better."

"And I want you to."

"But ... I ain't know if you got down like that."

"All you had to do was ask."

"I guess."

"Why didn't you ask?"

"Seemed like a funny thing to bring up. Embarrassin', too."

"Oh? How so?"

"Well, like I said, I ain't know if you got down like that and ... I ain't know if I was yo' type. If you *got* a type ... "

"A good brother with a good spirit and a good outlook on life? *You're* my type."

Antwan smiled. "And ... I ain't know how you might take a brutha like me steppin' to a brutha like you."

"And what kind of brothers are we?"

"You got this fly job at a design firm. I'm just managin' a Taco Bell."

"No one *just* manages such an operation. It takes a lot of know how, a lot of patience, and a *lot* of gumption."

"Gumption? What's that?"

"It means you're resourceful. I've *heard* you in action. You have to make sure the employees are on the job and on *their* job, make sure the customer is taken care of and happy, and make sure the higher-ups are happy about the bottom line. If I had to deal with all of that, I'd probably be coming home every night getting drunk."

Antwan chuckled.

"And, you worked your way up the ladder in three years— and did it *without* a college degree. *That's* sayin' something."

"There's another one. I ain't think you'd wanna get wit' somebody who ain't go to college."

"Why would you think that? I talk to you five days a week."

"Yeah, but talkin' to me and *talkin'* to me, they two diff'rent things. A lota bruthaz I try to holla at, they brush me off 'cause I ain't in that club."

"Hey, you're in a club, a class by yourself. Any brother who knows the real thing would be able to see that."

"Uh, thanks, man. But it ain't just about what I do but how I am. I ain't exactly, you know, proper like you."

"Proper?"

"Yeah. Like, the way you speak. The way you carry ya self."

"You got your own style, your own way. And that's good."

"But I don't talk perfect English."

"There's no such thing. Proper, maybe. But we all have our own ways of expressing ourselves."

"And ... you blind."

"OK. What does that have to do with anything?"

"Maybe nothin'. Maybe everything."

"What do you mean?"

"Well ... I thought, maybe you only get wit' other blind people."

"You ever heard of Stevie Wonder or Ray Charles being with other blind people?"

"Uh, nah."

"We usually don't pair up with each other."

"Why not?"

"I don't know. Maybe 'cause there can only be one invalid in the relationship." Ellington snickered.

His self-deprecating humor was dismissed by Antwan. "You ain't no invalid."

"I know. But getting two of us together ... depending on the people involved, that could be one pitiful pity party."

"Why?"

"Well, people come into relationships with so much baggage. But being blind or any number of so-called handicaps just magnifies that tenfold. So most of us probably figure, if we want a leg up in the situation, it's best to be with someone who can see. At least then you get to see the world through the eyes of someone who actually *can* see."

"You never been wit' somebody blind?"

"Oh, I have. But it didn't take long to figure out it wasn't for me."

"So, you seein' somebody right now?"

"Ha, if I was, *they'd* be here, right now. It's been about eight months."

"How long was y'all together?"

"Just over a year."

"How come it ain't work out?"

"Well ... he thought he could handle it. He realized he couldn't."

"Y'all don't speak?"

"We do. He's still a good friend."

"Then how come you ain't ask him to celebrate ya birthday?"

"We did, earlier today. He took me to lunch. Besides, I just didn't want to spend it with a friend; I wanted to spend it with someone I can get friendly with."

Ellington could feel him grin.

"You've never been with one of my kind before?"

"Nah."

"Never crossed your mind, huh?"

"Nah. Not 'til I met you."

"What do you find attractive about me?"

"You smart. And funny. Got a great personality."

"Hmph, just the things one wants to hear when asked what makes them *attractive*."

Antwan knocked Ellington's knee with his own. "I ain't finished. Anyway, I usually go for light-skinned bruthaz."

"Hmm ... I bet you have Hershey bar brown skin."

"Uh, yeah. How you know?"

"People usually find themselves attracted to their opposite. So, all a brother has to be is light-skinned to get you hot?"

"Nah, man. He gotta be hella-sexy. Like you."

"I am?"

"Yeah. You got a tight frame. And yo' ears ... they cute."

"My *ears* are cute?"

"Don't ask me how they can be cute, a'ight? They just is. Bite-size. Bet they'd be nice to nibble on."

"O-K ... "

"And them lips ... " Antwan stared at them. "*Man.*"

Ellington smiled; he licked his lips.

"And when you do that LL thang. *Day-um.*"

Ellington chuckled. "Did you think that, if you approached me, I might think you were doing it *because* I'm blind, that you'd see me as some sort of experiment?"

"Uh, yeah."

"I've been there. A couple of times. Mmm ... if you *did* feel that way, I don't think I'd mind that much."

"Why?"

"Because, having a brother like you experiment on me could be fun."

"Nah. It *will* be."

Ellington blushed.

"Uh ... ya know, you don't seem blind."

"Huh?"

"I mean, the way you talk about stuff. The way you break shit down. It's like ... you can see."

"One doesn't need eyes to see. I saw you, and I've never laid eyes on you."

"That's what I mean. You so ... perspective."

"Perceptive?"

"Yeah. Perceptive."

"Well, I've had to be. My other senses fill in for my sight."

"And how they do that?"

Ellington placed his left hand on Antwan's right thigh, and *squeezed*. "I can't tell you how; I have to show you."

Antwan's thigh—meaty, firm, warm—felt *good*. But Ellington began his exploration with Antwan's hands; they were the first body part of Antwan's he ever touched, that he was ever touched by. They were so velvety; they reminded Ellington of velour cloth. How could hands so large be so gentle, so strong yet so soft? Whenever he and Antwan shook hands or Antwan gripped or hugged him with them, he got the goosebumps.

Ellington got the goosebumps again when Antwan placed his right hand on top of Ellington's left. Ellington traced each of Antwan's long fingers, from the thumb to the pinky, with his own thumb, then his middle, then his pinky. Ellington repeated each step, but with the inside of his own palm. He traced the nail on each finger with his thumb, as his index served as support. Then he worked backwards, lightly massaging and pulling on each finger and finger tip, causing Antwan to breathe a little heavier and quicker.

Ellington turned Antwan's hand over and held it as his thumb circled the area from the wrist to the beginning of each finger. Antwan giggled when Ellington traced figure eights and let out faint sighs as Ellington massaged the middle of his palm. Those sighs became more pronounced when Ellington performed the same sensuous wrist wrap Jamie Foxx imitated on Regina King in *Ray*.

"Please come with me," Ellington requested, still holding his wrist by the thumb and index finger.

They stood, face to face. Antwan enclosed his right hand around Ellington's left. Ellington placed his right hand on Antwan's left pumped-up pec, clutching as he read his heartbeat, which began to pump furiously. Antwan did the same to him, and Ellington also had to catch up to his breath. Ellington's hand traveled slowly up to his neck, then tugged on his ear; Antwan did the same. Then Ellington's hand opened and cupped the back of Antwan's head ...

"*My, my, my,*" Ellington harmonized like Johnny Gill. To his delight, Antwan was bald. Well, not just bald, but super-buffed butterball bald. The kind of bald head that glistens in the sun, that is as glossy as glass. Ellington's paternal grandfather, also named Ellington, possessed such a head; he went hairless when Isaac Hayes made the look cool for Black men in the seventies. Even at the age of six, Ellington found himself enchanted by it. Watching PaPa shave and shine was the highlight of his visits to his grandparents' home.

One day, Ellington was outside the bathroom, perched in his usual spot and peeking inside, when ...

"Boy, I'm tired of you just standin' there. We gonna put you to work, too."

PaPa placed a gell in both of Ellington's palms and instructed him on how to rub it on and in. He performed the task fifty times, the final seventeen after he lost his sight. It made Ellington tingly all over, proof that he was, as his great aunt Vera remarked, "a little twinkly." Ever since then, Ellington has had a thing for bald men; most of his dates and both of his lovers were.

So a discovery like this called for both hands.

"Would you bow your head just a little, please?" Ellington asked.

Antwan eagerly complied.

"Thank you." Ellington released his other hand from Antwan's grip and placed all ten of his finger tips on his head. He lightly yet deliberately pressed, pressed in, then pressed down, kneading the head like dough, as Antwan's entire body followed, left to right, up and down, round and round.

"*Man.* That feels so *good,*" Antwan breathed.

"It sure does."

Ellington worked on the head five more minutes, then brushed Antwan's rectangular-shaped forehead, tapped his temples, smoothed over his eyebrows, pinched his cheeks, and then made another discovery: dimples! They both chuckled as Ellington playfully poked them. Ellington's thumbs outlined Antwan's goatee as both index fingers brushed Antwan's nose. Then Ellington paused as he prepared to finally touch what is, for him, the gateway to a man's soul: the lips. One is most vulnerable, open, naked when their lips kiss another's—which is why, he reasons, some men, non-hetero especially, frown down on or refuse to do it. You *inhale* the essence of the other, even more than when you are inside of them or vice versa. Whatever pretense, whatever defense, whatever invisible wall one may have up disappears once the mouths merge, and you *really* experience the person they are.

Antwan's lips were just as Ellington prayed they would be—very thick, the top curved up, the bottom slightly folded down. Always parted, always enticing. Ellington's right pinky coated them like a tube of Chapstick. The tip of Antwan's tongue would dart forward and make contact with the pinky every time Ellington returned to the very center of Antwan's bottom lip. They exhaled a groan in unison.

"You are *so* beautiful," Ellington complimented.

"I am?"

"Yes." Ellington felt him tense up.

"Ain't nodoby ever told me that."

"What, are *they* blind?"

Antwan giggled.

On the ninth pinky-lip go 'round, Ellington couldn't take it anymore. He firmly held Antwan's face and, lathering up his own lips, went in for a landing.

"Hold up, man," Antwan politely yet sternly demanded, pushing him back. "I gotta check you out first."

Ellington was disappointed; he was *dying* to taste his lips. But ... *why should I have all the fun? Fair is fair, right? Hmm ... no other man wanted to return that favor.* There were those goosebumps ...

Antwan had paid close attention. He followed the blueprint Ellington set forth: same body parts, same sequence, same plays, same precision. But he added a couple of twists: blowing in Ellington's right ear and nibbling on its lobe.

Ellington lost it, both times, literally jumping out of his shoes. "*Mph.* What you do *that* for?" he shrieked.

"What, ya don't like it?" Antwan snickered.

"You know I do. You're cheating."

"My bad."

"*You're* bad."

Antwan caressed the left side of Ellington's face. Ellington knew *it was time*; he reached out with his left hand, let it travel up the left side of Antwan's chest and over his shoulder, until it was palming the back of Antwan's dome. They slowly moved in. After watching Ellington arch his head to the left, Antwan followed suit. Their heads leaned in, noses touching. They paused. Their lips reached out and met.

ZAP!

Ellington felt the same shock to his system when he shook Antwan's hand for the first time, when he heard him laugh for the first time, when he hugged him for the first time.

They kissed. And kissed. And kissed. And kissed. Lightly yet longingly. They carefully explored the other's lips. But Ellington was fixated on Antwan's bottom lip, which at one point he'd captured in his own mouth.

"Ha, ain't you ever gonna let it go?" Antwan managed to ask, still in his grip.

"Oh. Sorry." He released him from his lip but not from his grip, which he tightened around the waist. "It just tastes *so* good."

Antwan rubbed up against him, his arms flung over Ellington's shoulders. "It does?"

"Yes."

"What do it taste like?"

He sucked on it again. "Like butterscotch—with a hint of cherry."

"That's a Jolly Rancher."

"The butterscotch is *you*."

"You like butterscotch?"

"I *love* butterscotch."

The kissing became more ... well, sloppy. They hungrily slobbered all over and inside of the other's mouth. Antwan would catch and gnaw on Ellington's tongue, which had Ellington out of his shoes, again (this time he kept them off; Antwan followed suit). Ellington had been sniffing him out all night but now the heat they were generating was making Antwan's aroma so potent he was feeling a bit of a buzz. So he finally inquired ...

"What *is* that you're wearing?"

"Huh?" Antwan didn't hear him; he was a bit buzzy himself.

"Your cologne. Or is that you?"

"It's this potion I get from a brutha up in Harlem."

"A potion? No wonder it's putting a serious spell on me."

"It is?"

"Yes. It's always had me hypnotized. But now? *Whew.*"

Antwan laughed.

"What's it called?"

Antwan snickered. "Eat It Raw."

Ellington stopped snacking on his neck. "You're kidding."

"Nah."

"For real?"

"Yeah."

Ellington licked his lips. "I promise—I *will*."

After Antwan's tongue found his ear again, Ellington took off the perfect gentleman gloves and let his hands slide down to Antwan's booty, which, according to his calculations, was very high, very round, and very bubbly.

"*Mmmm*," Antwan growled.

Ellington squeezed each cheek like he would a grape-fruit. Thumped them as if they were melons. Rubbed them as if they were crytsal balls that could reveal his future. Well, in a way, they would: Antwan stopped purring and asked in a low voice, his lips in Ellington's right ear ...

"You like that azz?"

"*Yes*," Ellington hissed.

"You want some of that azz?"

"No. I want it *all*." Ellington whacked both cheeks.

"*Uh.* Then come on." Antwan's tongue darted in and out of his ear. "Take it. Take it all."

How ironic that, at that very moment, Gerald Alston was pleading: *Here is my love, take me where you want to ...* Ellington couldn't have programmed his iPod (which was in his Bose Sound Dock) any perfectly.

There was only one thing Ellington could say, also in Antwan's ear. "Let's take this to the bedroom."

Antwan answered with a *moan*. Then ... "Whatcha doin'?"

"What does it feel like? I'm carrying you there."

"Uh, you sure this a good idea?"

"Of course it is. No one knows this apartment better than I do." It's been his home for six years. Besides, he'd choreographed this particular moment in his mind, in his dreams, in his *day* dreams for months.

"But ain't I heavy?"

"Yes. But the right kind of heavy." And he was. They were the same height (5' 11") and had similar builds. Ellington weighed 170; because he was buff, Ellington deciphered that Antwan was close to 185.

Antwan was surprised and impressed: they made it to the bedroom without bumping into anything, or Ellington losing his balance. Ellington laid Antwan down diagonally—

his feet dangling, his head at the foot of the bed. Why there? Because that's where Ellington positioned four throw pillows. Yes, Ellington had prepared; he was *ready*. The red light was on. The scent of the wild raspberry candle, encased in a fire/ shatter-proof jar on the window sill, filled the room. The hot massage oil, condoms and lube were on the nightstand. Two towels sat on top of the dresser. And Ellington had on as few items of clothing as possible: a silver silk shirt (unbuttoned at the top; he wanted Antwan to undo the rest), black slacks, and no socks. Oh, and no underwear. He never leaves the house without 'em but knew they'd just get in the way, add one unnecessary step to the itinerary. He's sure his hard-on was very visible for most of the evening, especially when Antwan placed his hand on Ellington's shoulder as they transfered to the sofa.

Antwan had a surprise for Ellington: *He* wasn't wearing underwear, either. As Ellington unzipped and pulled down his pants, the dick popped out and popped Ellington in the nose.

"I guess he's really glad to see me, huh?"

Antwan chuckled.

They switched positions. After taking off Ellington's shirt, Antwan wondered out loud: "Should I take off yo' glasses?"

Ellington hesitated. "Yes."

His slacks were still on but Ellington felt completely nude. He only removed his glasses when he showered or retired for the night. *Seeing* that he really couldn't see has been the deal breaker for many men he's been interested in. But he got the feeling that this time it would be different. And his intuition didn't fail him: Antwan carefully placed them on the nightstand, cupped Ellington's chin, then kissed each closed eye. Ellington smiled; he could feel Antwan smiling, too.

Antwan slid off Ellington's pants and then ... nothing. Silence. *Why is he so quiet? Does he not like what he sees? I'm not as tight or muscular as him, but I'm not a twig either. Is he thinking of a way to retreat?* Antwan answered those silent queries when he tackled him, shoving his tongue into Ellington's mouth. Ellington didn't mind. They resumed making out. Ellington couldn't believe Antwan was there, and *bare*, after so many nights wishing he was. It was so much better than any dream he had, and more than he could ever have dreamed of. He kept pinching Antwan (who didn't mind) and pinching himself to make sure he wasn't. He loved having Antwan in his arms, having Antwan on top of him, having Antwan's hands all over him, having hand*fuls* of Antwan ... just *having* him. They rolled and jostled from one end of the bed to the other.

After Ellington polished Antwan's bald head with his tongue, received nourishment from Antwan's pointy nipples ("I've always *loved* chocolate milk"), outlined Antwan's pecs and the ridges of his eight-pack like he did his fingers, and puckered his navel (which drove Antwan wild) ... it was time to go *there*.

He continued making his way downtown. Antwan's apricot-smelling pubic hairs were tickling his nostrils when ...

"Hold up, E." Antwan stopped him by his shoulders.

Damn. He's putting on the brakes, again. Did he change his mind? Wouldn't be the first time it's happened. But he can't turn me off in the middle of turning me on ... "Yes?"

"I ... I gotta tell you somethin'."

Ellington eased up on Antwan's left. "What is it?"

"Uh ... "

Ellington sensed him looking down.

"I ... I got HIV."

Ellington shrugged. "OK."

Antwan looked up. "You heard what I said?"

"Yes."

"Well ... "

"Well what?"

"That don't bother you?"

"No. Why should it?"

"It ... bothers most bruthaz I tell."

"I ain't most brothers."

"But, bein' wit' me ... it can put you at risk."

"I know that. But not if we're careful."

"You mean ... you still wanna?"

"*Hell yeah.*"

Antwan laughed.

Ellington reached for and pinched his left nipple. "I'm already taking a risk."

"You mean, you positive, too?"

"No, I'm not. As far as I know. My last test was three months ago."

"Then whatcha mean?"

"Inviting you into my home. Inviting you into my bed. Inviting you into my world. It's a big step."

Antwan placed his right hand on Ellington's thigh, tenderly stroking it. Then he suddenly yanked on Ellington's dick. "Not as big as *this*."

Ellington jumped a few inches up *off* the bed, gasping for air.

Then Antwan swallowed him. *Whole.* Ellington was beside himself. Outside of himself. And couldn't control himself. His body began to convulse, his arms waving erratically.

"*Mercy,*" Ellington shouted.

His dick expanded inside of Antwan's mouth, which, to Ellington's shock *and* joy, just expanded to accomodate it. And, all the while, Antwan sucked on it as if it were a Jolly Rancher.

"*Mercy,*" Ellington testified again.

Ellington wasn't a member of the double digit club but he had girth. Most of the men he'd been with, including his ex, had to get used to him, and even when they did, they were unable to take it all (in the mouth, anyway). But Antwan ... he acted as if this was his hundreth time up at this bat. He bobbed up and down as his tongue circled and put pressure on the shaft, never once releasing it from his hold. All Ellington could do was, once again, shout ...

"*Mercy.*"

Ellington placed his right hand on the bed and his left fingertips on the top of Antwan's head. As Antwan swallowed down, Ellington thrust forward in a circular motion. Antwan *loved* that; to Ellington's amazement, he was able to exclaim "*Ah yeah*" with all that dick in his mouth. Antwan amped up his sucking speed, while fondling Ellington's balls.

The shock gone, Ellington fucked Antwan's face for a bit, then shifted down onto his right side (never interrupting Antwan's wondrous penis pig-out), and grasped Antwan's dick with his left hand.

"*Uh-uh-uh,*" Antwan stuttered.

Ellington played with Antwan's doorknob first, wrapping his tongue around it.

"*Aaah,*" Antonie muttered.

Unlike Ellington, Antwan *was* a member of the double digit club (or at least close to it). His dick grew around four inches in under a minute—and Ellington hadn't gotten past the head! Ellington held it like an ear of corn and puckered the sides like a fish, from head to base.

"*Ohohohoh,*" Antwan almost sang.

Ellington swallowed him half.

"*Hhhhhhoh,*" Antwan huffed.

Then almost whole.

"*Ye-ah,*" Antwan puffed.

Then whole.

"*Aaaaw shit,*" Antwan snarled, mounting upwards and on top of Ellington. Since Antwan's dick pointed diagonally at a thrity degree angle, Ellington was in the perfect position to deep throat—which Ellington did.

It was *the* best 69 action Ellington ever had. Antwan, too.

Ellington was almost on the verge when Antwan stopped and pulled away from him. Antwan could tell Ellington was bewildered.

"Man, I don't want us cumin' just yet. I gotta hop on that phat dick first."

Ellington *grinned.*

Antwan figured that the contour pillow was positioned at the head of the bed for just that purpose, so he guided Ellington there. Not a second after Ellington got comfortable, Antwan booty bum-rushed him in the face.

"*C'mon, E, eat dat azz,*" Antwan demanded, on his knees with his palms on the bed, wiggling it at him.

"*My pleasure.*"

Taste, baste, and lay waste to the booty—those are a few of Ellington's favorite things. No, his top three. So Antwan didn't have to tell him twice; it truly *would* be his pleasure to anal-yze him.

Ellington *grabbed* the cheeks. He *spread* them—causing a soft squeak to emanate from Antwan—and went a sniffin'.

Antwan shivered. "*Wooh.*"

Ellington blew on the hole.

Antwan quivered. "*Ay ya.*"

Ellington drew figure eights again, this time around and on the hole with his tongue.

Antwan twirled his booty in synch. "*Ooh ooh ooh.*"

Ellington jabbed his tongue in and out.

"C'mon, now, E, stop tea-sin' me," Antwan pleaded, pounding his fists on the bed.

Ellington stopped teasing him.

"Uh-huh. Yeah. Git cha face all up in ma place," Antwan chanted a half-dozen times, as if he were a rapper.

Of course, Ellington *did* get his face all up in Antwan's place, *and* kept his promise: he ate it *raw*. He chowed down like the Tazmanian Devil. And why wouldn't he, since the ass was succulently sweet, like a mango.

Antwan flung it, locking his beefy thighs around Ellington's rib cage and pinning him against the headboard (Ellington didn't mind being trapped; if necessary, he'd just eat his way out).

Then the booty started *calling* Ellington. It clapped on Ellington's face: *Pat-a-pat. Pat-a-pat. Pat-a-pat.* How fitting that Toni Braxton was vocalizing what Ellington was thinking: *Talk dirty to me baby, with-out talk-ing at all ...*

"Damn, Ant. That azz is sayin' my name." Ellington smacked both cheeks so hard that the vibration traveled from the bed to the nightstand, knocking the tube of hot oil onto the floor.

Antwan was still in Jay-Z mode. *"Then c'mon, E, wrap it so you can tap it."* He swiped up the lube and flicked up the opening. He took Ellington's left hand and greased his fingertips. He got on all fours.

Ellington poked his thumb in and out of the hole.

Antwan's azz rose higher. *"Mmm."*

Ellington worked his middle finger in.

Antwan pushed back. *"Mmm-hmm."*

Ellington worked the middle and forefingers in.

Antwan pushed back some more. *"Mmm-hmm, mmm-hmm."*

Ellington double finger-fucked him, slowly, then with a vengeance.

Antwan flailed the azz like crazy. *"Oh, oh, oh."*

Ellington had to have it. He reached for and ripped open the condom wrapper. Antwan watched as he carefully sat it on top of his dick's head and rolled it down.

"Man. You a pro," Antwan complimented.

"I'm a pro?"

"Yeah. I always hafta wrap up the other kat, 'cause he don't know how. Or he take so fuckin' long gettin' it on I almost fall asleep."

Ellington chuckled. "Really? Wow. That's ... scary. Every man should know how, especially if he is Black."

Antwan sighed. "There you go."

"There I go what?"

"Doin' that, and sayin' that."

"What?"

"You get me burnin'."

Ellington reached out for him with his left hand. "Hope you don't mind a little more fire."

Antwan took it. "I don't."

Antwan placed the contour pillow behind Ellington, who sat up at the head of the bed; he positioned the throw pillows a few inches behind himself, one on top of each other. Antwan squatted down as Ellington placed his hands under Antwan's thighs, to keep him steady. Antwan positioned Ellington's dick up against his opening, pushing down.

"Aaah," they grunted, as the head penetrated Antwan.

Antwan eased down, then up, repeating the steps and taking in a little more of Ellington each time. On the sixth go-down, he had all of Ellington inside.

"Oh," Antwan cried out.

"*Mmm*, you feel *so* good, Ant." Then *he* tripped off like Jay-Z. "*Real* tight, and *just* right. So, don't resist; just submit." Ellington kissed him. He enclosed him in his arms.

Antwan relaxed and rested his elbows on Ellington's shoulders and his right hand on Ellington's back. He ran his left through Ellington's hair, and began to swerve the ass left to right.

"*Aaaah. That's it, Ant. Go on 'n' claim it.*"

Antwan lifted up and rocked forward, like a horse on a merry go-round. Ellington met him every time he came down with a curled thrust, which always elicited a growl from both.

"*Work it on up in me, E, mph.*"

"*With pleasure, Ant. With pleasure.*"

Those growls grew in volume as Antwan locked his lower legs underneath Ellington's thighs, and Ellington spanked his azz.

"*Uh-huh, drum da bootay, E.*"

"*With pleasure.*"

As Antwan bounced, Ellington bucked. As Antwan jigged, Ellington jiggled. Antwan performed surgery on Ellington's right ear. Ellington helped himself to some more chocolate milk.

Then Ellington pushed them forward; his arms extended and his fists punched into the mattress. Antwan landed on his shoulders, the throw pillows providing a cushion under his waist. He bent his knees in and out. He hoisted his lower legs up; his feet were parallel to the bed.

Ellington *drilled* him.

"*Uh-huh, dunk that dick in me, E, yeah.*"

"*With pleasure.*"

Ellington dunked faster and harder; Antwan squealed higher and louder.

"*Go on, E, do da day-um thang.*"

"With pleasure."

For Ellington, there's *no* sound in the world like one's balls slapping up against another man's ass. *Plap, plap, plap.* You recognize it instantly. When you hear it, you know *it is goin' down.* At one point, that was the only sound filling the room (not counting the heavy panting and gruff sighs). Neither one of them *said* a word; none were needed. Ellington's dick was doing all the talking. It was Ellington's turn to claim it.

The sex was neo acid jazz. Ellington was a little bit soul, Antwan a little bit hip-hop. They both delivered their own funk. And the *plap, plap, plap* was the rhythm track, with the bed-knockin' on the wall—*dum, dum, dum*—adding a little percussion to the mix.

Something's burning, Ellington thought. *Did I leave the burner on under the rice?*

Then he realized ... *it's us.*

Yes, *they* were burning. Smoldering. Simmering. Sizzling.

It had to be a hundred degrees in the bedroom. And it had to be a hundred degrees inside Antwan. Hot. *So* hot. But not too hot. The right kind of hot. And they—one big, steaming, boiling pot—were about to blow their tops.

"Oh, Ant, I'm gonna cum!"

"Then cum wit' it, E. Cum oooon."

They beat the other's meat, screaming the other's name over and over, decorating their chests with the other's sticky wicky. They hunched forward, their foreheads banging. They laughed while trying to catch their breath.

Antwan grabbed the towels. He wiped Ellington off.

"Thank you."

"You welcome."

Ellington reciprocated with the other.

"Thanks."

"You're welcome."

They laid down, Ellington on his left side, Antwan his right. Antwan inserted his right leg between Ellington's thighs. Ellington pulled him in closer. They leaned in, forehead to forehead. Ellington clenched Antwan's left butt cheek with his right hand.

Ellington began whistling the "Happy Birthday" song.

"I guess you enjoyed yo' present."

"To borrow a phrase, *hella yeah*."

They laughed.

Antwan checked himself out. "I think you left fingerprints on me."

"And probably a few other marks."

"Mmm-hmm. But ya missed a few spots."

Ellington thought of the massage oil. "Then I got some more work to do." His right hand moved up Antwan's torso, down to his thigh, then back again.

Antwan sighed. "Don't be lookin' at me like that."

"*Look* at you?" Ellington snickered.

"Yeah, *look* at me."

"How can *I* look at *you?*"

"You been doin' it all night. You know how you do."

"How?"

"It ... it's the way ya mouth bunches up, like you about to smile but you ain't. And ya nostrils, they kinda flare up. Then ya lips, they open up a bit. And ya tongue kinda peeks out. You be lookin' at me."

He noticed. "You don't like it when I look at you like that?"

"I ain't say I don't like it. I'm just sayin' ... "

"You just sayin' it makes you *burn*."

He giggled. "I guess."

"You *know*. You still doubt me?"

"Doubt you? I ain't doubt you."

"Yes you did. All seeing people doubt those who can't."

"Man ... that ain't fair."

"May not be fair, but it's true."

"I ... I ain't doubt *you*."

"Maybe not me, but you did doubt how I could make you feel."

"Uh ... I admit it. I did."

"Seeing is not always believing."

"Nah it ain't. *Feelin'* is."

"It sure is, Babe."

"Babe?"

"Oh. Sorry. It just ... felt natural. You don't like that nickname?"

"Nah, nah. I like it." Antwan moved in closer. "Now I gotta come up wit' one for you."

"I think you already did."

"What?"

"Mother-fucker."

"Huh?"

"You called me that twenty-six times during ... "

"You did a count?"

"I couldn't help it. You say it with ... with such ... "

"Gumption?"

Ellington chuckled. "Uh, in a way, yes. It's so ... so ... *nasty*. And *sexy*. You can be so fresh."

"You liked it?"

"You know it."

"But that can't be yo' aka."

"You'll come up with one. I'm sure I'll like it. Oh, and just for the record: I've never actually fucked a mother before."

"You funny."

"But the right kind of funny. What about you?"

"What about me?"

"Have—or do you—fuck mothers?"

"Uh, I been wit' a few females. Ain't been wit' one in a long time."

"How long is long?"

"Like, six years."

"That is a long time. Any plans on making a return engagement?"

"Nah. I was only wit' 'em 'cause ... you know ... "

"Playing it straight?"

"Yeah. Now, I'm only a man's man."

Ellington tapped his azz. "Hmph. I know you are."

They kissed. Antwan melded into him, his head finding just the right spot on Ellington's chest. Ellington settled on his back. His left hand roped Antwan's waist; his right explored the indentations on Antwan's ripped back. He placed a kiss on the very top of Antwan's head. They breathed together. They drifted off to sleep.

Ellington was sleeping *good* when he was awakened by ... *is that crying?*

"Are you alright, Babe?"

"Uh, yeah." Antwan's voice quivered.

"You don't sound like it."

He choked up. "I ... I ... "

"What's wrong? You can tell me."

"I ... I just wish you could really see me."

Ellington's right hand wiped away the tears. "Me too, Babe. Me, too." He rocked him until he heard that steady breathing again.

Antwan woke Ellington up the second time with butterfly kisses on his eyelids. *Ah ... sunshine on my face and sunshine in my arms; what a way to start the day.*

"*Mmm.* Good morning, Babe."

"Good mornin'."

They lip-locked.

Ellington sucked on Antwan's bottom lip. "Are you hungry?"

"Not as hungry as you."

"Ha, sorry. Just can't help myself."

"It's a'ight."

"What do you feel like eating?"

"I don't know."

"I know what *I* feel like eating." Ellington shoved his middle finger in his azz.

It was Antwan's turn to jump two inches up off the bed. "*Ooh.*" Antwan nudged him in the left side. "You nasty."

"May-be. But you know as well as I that you won't object when I stick my tongue up that booty." That finger still in place, he whacked the azz with the other hand.

Antwan shuddered, and Ellington felt *his* goosebumps as they popped up.

"*Uh-huh.*" Ellington chuckled. "The best part of waking up—*besides* waking up—is having cakes like these in my cup."

They laughed. They kissed.

"Thanks for being with me last night, Babe. And this morning."

"Thanks for askin' me. I can be wit' you tonite, too."

Ellington was stunned. "Tonight?"

"Yeah. I already got my toothbrush and stuff. But I hafta run home and get my work clothes for tomorrow."

"So ... you want to stay the night again?"

"Yeah."

"Really?"

"Yeah. If you want me to."

Ellington nodded yes. "I most certainly do. But … what does this mean?"

"Whatcha mean?"

"What is it that we are … getting into?"

"I don't know. I guess we gettin' into … *somethin'*."

Ellington nodded. "OK. But … can you handle this?"

"Judgin' from them sounds comin' outa you, I can handle *this*"—he grabbed the dick—"wit' no problem."

Ellington trembled; his woody got more wooden. "Now, don't get—"

"*Cock*-y?"

They laughed.

Ellington sighed. "I'm talking about … this."

"This?"

"You know. My situation."

"You ain't no situation."

Ellington *exhaled*. "No. I'm not."

"I ain't sure if I can. But … I know I ain't just feelin' you, I'm feelin' good about you."

"I feel the same way about you."

Antwan beamed; Ellington did, too. They kissed.

Antwan ran his fingers through Ellington's hair. "I'm willin' to take a chance. How 'bout you?"

Ellington squeezed him *tight*. "I already am."

A SUMTHIN'S EXTRA ...

"Errol Comes Out"
from the upcoming *B-Boy Blues* novel, *Men of the House*

In the following excerpt, Raheim Errol Rivers III—the 15-year-old son of Raheim ("Pooquie") Rivers—tells his best friends, Sidney ("Sid") and Monroe ("Roe"), about his father and godfather, Mitchell ("Little Bit") Crawford, reuniting

Sid didn't seem surprised by Errol's revelation; he responded with his trademark "OK, next," shrug. He didn't get worked up over much.

Roe, on the other hand, was catatonic. It was the first time Errol had ever seen his mouth open so wide and he wasn't stuffing it with food.

"Man, close your mouth before something flies in it," Sid advised him.

He didn't (or, maybe couldn't).

Errol nudged Roe in the left arm with his right elbow. "Roe? You alright?"

Errol knew Roe would be the hardest to lay the news on. Even though Roe had gotten used to being around and speaking with Mitchell about being gay, finding out Raheim wasn't straight and that he and Mitchell had been and are once again a couple would, as Mitchell predicted, "rock his world."

Or, rock him into a petrified state.

Errol, Roe and Sid were in Roe's attic, which subbed as their "treehouse" the entire three years they've been best friends. Errol was seated between them on the red velvet sofa, so he didn't have to look either of them in the eye as he shared the secrets.

Errol nudged Roe, again. "Say something."

Roe sighed heavily. *"Wow."*

Sid chuckled. "Well, that's something."

Roe glanced at Errol, in disbelief. "Ya Pops is ... "

"Bisexual," Errol finished for him.

"And *him* ... and Mr. C?"

"Yup."

He sighed heavily, again. *"Wow."*

Errol giggled.

"So ... " Roe began. "He likes women and men?"

Errol nodded. "He's attracted to both women and men."

"Is he still attracted to women?"

"Of course," Sid interjected. "That's what *bi*sexual means."

"But ... how can he be attracted to both men and women at the same time?"

"Can you turn your attraction to females off like a light switch?" Errol questioned.

"No. But I don't have another option on the table."

"Just because he's attracted to both sexes at the same time doesn't mean he's with both at the same time."

"And, clearly, he's not," added Sid.

Roe considered what they said. "Hmm ... I guess if I was bi, ain't no way I could be with just one at a time. I'd be greedy."

They all laughed.

"Uh, how long they been ... together?"

"Off and on, for like ten years."

"Ten years?"

"Yeah."

"You mean, they been ... together since you was *five?*"

"Yup."

"Damn. When did he tell you?"

"My Dad told me the whole story when I was eight. But I knew before then."

"You did?"

"Yup."

"When?"

"I guess ... the first time I met Uncle Mitch."

"Really?"

"Yeah. They didn't exactly hide it. I could sense what they were feeling but I didn't know what to call it. I mean, I was so young. But I knew he made my Dad happy."

Roe marinated on that for a moment, then peered at Sid. "Man, I guess you were right."

Errol turned to Sid. "About what?"

"At your birthday party. I noticed how they were looking at each other."

"How were they looking at each other?"

"Like ... they were in love."

Errol observed this, too—especially when they'd *gaze* if the other wasn't looking. Since Sid is very observant, it didn't surprise Errol that he caught it, too. *I wonder if anyone else at the party noticed?*

"I told him he was seein' things," Roe admitted.

"And what else did you say?" Sid asked.

"I ... don't remember," Roe mumbled.

"Yes you do," Sid shot back.

"Ain't no way Mr. R could be ... like *that*," Roe confessed, somewhat embarrassed.

Errol laughed. "As opposed to being like *this*."

Sid and Roe laughed, too.

"And why couldn't he be?" Errol inquired.

"You know ... he so ... so ... "

Errol filled in that blank. "Manly."

"Yeah. Not that Mr. C ain't. It's just ... if you saw ya pops walkin' down the street, you would just assume he was straight."

"*You* would just assume he's straight," Sid corrected.

"So, if you didn't know my Uncle Mitch and you saw him walking down the street, you'd assume he was gay?"

"Mmm ... may-be."

"You can't assume anything about anyone. People who are gay—or bisexual—don't have to look or act a certain way."

"I know. But, sometimes, they be wearin' the gay on their sleeve."

Errol was floored by that one. "'They be wearin' the gay on their sleeve?' Is that a new homo-ism you heard your pops say?" Roe's father is very homophobic and has some looney ideas about gays and lesbians ("If you let a homo touch you, you'll get AIDS.") If he knew that one of his son's best friends had Same Gender Loving parents, he'd implode.

"Nah. I heard a dude say that on TV the other day about that show, *Queer As Folk.*"

"It's not about wearing it; it's about being it," Errol explained. "And some are just a little more ... open about it."

"Yeah, just like you are a little more open about your heterosexuality," Sid observed, pointing at Roe.

"Whatcha mean?"

"What's your favorite subject?"

"The ladies!" Roe exclaimed.

"Right. And you never let anyone forget it. It's 24-7 with you, non-stop."

"But all dudes are like that."

Sid pointed to himself and Errol. "We're not."

"Ha, that's because you only been with one, and E's been with none."

"Oh, yeah, I guess that makes you the Casanova of the posse," Sid cracked sarcastically.

A lightbulb came on over Roe's head. "*Man!* Is he one of them homo thugs Mr. C was talkin' about?"

"Huh?" Errol responded, puzzled.

"Mr. C said he dated homo thugs. I bet ya pops was one of them."

"I don't know, you'd have to ask him."

"You know he will," Sid snickered under his breath.

Roe continued with the queries. "Is he movin' in?"

"He already has."

"You wanted him to move in?"

"Yeah."

"Man ... that's gonna mess up our plan."

"What plan?"

"You know: Operation Over-Easy."

Operation Over-Easy, or Getting Over-Easy on Mitchell. Roe and Sid's fathers were in the home and could be strict (Sid's parents are Jehovah's Witnesses and just gave him permission to officially date his girlfriend, Juliet—who has been his sweetheart since they were both *seven*). Mitchell could also be stern but his repoire with them was more of an older brother than a guardian. He allowed them a little more lattitude (such as granting them an hour past curfew). Could Raheim entering the picture on a full-time basis change all of that?

Errol didn't believe so. "It won't be a problem. My Dad is real cool."

Roe contemplated his next question. "Uh ... are you scared?"

"Scared of what?"

"You know ... that ... you might end up ... "

Sid became flustered. "Man, you know better than that. Like the Black, the gay—or the bi—don't rub off."

"I'm just sayin'. If it's really how you born and it's in the genes ... it could run in the family."

Errol had never given that possibility much thought, but it always seemed to be a major concern for others. "And what if it did? Does that mean we can't be friends anymore?"

"Nah, nah, that ain't what I'm sayin'," Roe protested.

"You sure? 'Cause that sounds like where you're going."

"You my boi; ain't nothin' gonna change that. But ... if you was like ya Pops ... I mean, it's hard enough bein' Black. From what Mr. C says, it's doubly hard bein' Black and gay. I guess it would be the same bein' Black and bi."

Sid nudged Roe. "Looks like you got something else to ask Mr. R about."

They all chuckled.

Roe exhaled deeply. "*Man.* You knocked me out with that one, bruh. When you said you wanted to talk to us, I didn't think you were gonna say something like *that.*"

"What were you expecting me to say?"

"That you finally plan on gettin' with Max," Roe stated as if it were obvious.

Errol and Sid smiled at each other.

Sid tapped his right temple. "See. Females. Always on the brain."

ABOUT THE AUTHOR

James Earl Hardy is the author of the best-selling *B-Boy Blues* series: *B-Boy Blues* (1994), praised as "the first gay hip-hop love story" and a 1995 Lambda Literary Award Finalist; *2nd Time Around* (1996); *If Only For One Nite* (1997), an American Library Association Gay Novel of the Year Honoree; *The Day Eazy-E Died* (2001); *Love The One You're With* (2002); and *A House Is Not a Home* (2005). The seventh installment, "Is It Still Jood To Ya?", is featured in the short story collection *Visible Lives: Three Stories in Tribute to E. Lynn Harris* (2010). The series chronicles the relationship between a journalist from Brooklyn and a homeboy-bike messenger from Harlem. A film version of *B-Boy Blues* is in development.

Mr. Hardy has also penned biographies on filmmaker Spike Lee and pop music group Boyz II Men. His first theatrical production, *Confessions of a Homo Thug Porn Star*—a one-man show about adult film star Tiger Tyson—won the Downtown Urban Theater Festival's 2010 Best Short Prize.

In addition, Mr. Hardy is an award-winning entertainment feature writer and music/cultural critic. A 1993 honors graduate of Columbia University's Graduate School of Journalism, his byline has appeared in *Entertainment Weekly, Essence, Newsweek, The Source, Vibe, The Village Voice,* and *The Washington Post.* His essay on disco/dance legend Sylvester, "Living Proof," was a 2005 GLAAD Media Award Finalist.

Mr. Hardy has received Lifetime Achievement Awards from Gay Men of African Descent (GMAD) and the Hispanic Black Gay Coalition (HBGC). Born and raised in the Bedford-Stuyvesant section of Brooklyn, New York, he lives in Manhattan.